THE BRITISH BARBARIANS

A HILL-TOP NOVEL

GRANT ALLEN

The British Barbarians

Grant Allen

PO Box 2211
Fairfield, IA 52556
www.1stworldlibrary.org
First Edition

LCCN: 2004195305

Softcover ISBN: 1-4218-0136-1
Hardcover ISBN: 1-4218-0036-5
eBook ISBN: 1-4218-0236-8

The British Barbarians
contributed by Tim, Ed & Rodney
in support of
1st World Library Literary Society

INTRODUCTION

Which every reader of this book is requested to read before beginning the story.

This is a Hill-top Novel. I dedicate it to all who have heart enough, brain enough, and soul enough to understand it.

What do I mean by a Hill-top Novel? Well, of late we have been flooded with stories of evil tendencies: a Hill-top Novel is one which raises a protest in favour of purity.

Why have not novelists raised the protest earlier? For this reason. Hitherto, owing to the stern necessity laid upon the modern seer for earning his bread, and, incidentally, for finding a publisher to assist him in promulgating his prophetic opinions, it has seldom happened that writers of exceptional aims have been able to proclaim to the world at large the things which they conceived to be best worth their telling it. Especially has this been the case in the province of fiction. Let me explain the situation. Most novels nowadays have to run as serials through magazines or newspapers; and the editors of these periodicals are timid to a degree which outsiders would hardly believe with regard to the fiction they admit into their pages. Endless spells surround them. This story or episode would annoy their Catholic readers; that one would repel their Wesleyan Methodist subscribers; such an incident is unfit for the perusal of the young person; such another would drive away the offended British matron. I do not myself believe there is any real ground for this excessive and, to be quite frank, somewhat ridiculous timidity. Incredible as it may seem to the ordinary editor, I am of opinion that it would be possible to tell the truth, and yet preserve the circulation. A first-class journal does not really suffer because two or three formalists or two or three bigots among its thousands of subscribers give it up for six weeks in a pet of ill-temper - and then take it on again. Still, the effect remains: it is almost impossible to get a novel printed in an English journal unless it is warranted to contain nothing at all to which anybody, however narrow, could possibly object, on any grounds whatever, religious, political, social, moral, or aesthetic. The romance that appeals to the average editor must say or hint at nothing at all that is not universally believed and received by everybody everywhere in this realm of Britain. But literature, as Thomas Hardy says with truth, is mainly the expression of souls in revolt. Hence the antagonism between literature and journalism.

Why, then, publish one's novels serially at all? Why not appeal at once to the outside public, which has few such prejudices? Why not deliver one's message direct to those who are ready to consider it or at least to hear it? Because, unfortunately, the serial rights of a novel at the present day are three times as valuable, in money worth, as the final book rights. A man who elects to publish direct, instead of running his story through the columns of a newspaper, is forfeiting, in other words, three-quarters of his income. This loss the prophet who cares for his mission could cheerfully endure, of course, if only the diminished income were enough for him to live upon. But in order to write, he must first eat. In my own case, for example, up till the time when I published The Woman who Did, I could never live on the proceeds of direct publication; nor could I even secure a publisher who would consent to aid me in introducing to the world what I thought most important for it. Having now found such a publisher - having secured my mountain - I am prepared to go on delivering my message from its top, as long as the world will consent to hear it. I will willingly forgo the serial value of my novels, and forfeit three-quarters of the amount I might otherwise earn, for the sake of uttering the truth that is in me, boldly and openly, to a perverse generation.

For this reason, and in order to mark the distinction between these books which are really mine - my own in thought, in spirit, in teaching - and those which I have produced, sorely against my will, to satisfy editors, I propose in future to add the words, "A Hill-top Novel," to every one of my stories which I write of my own accord, simply and solely for the sake of embodying and enforcing my own opinions.

Not that, as critics have sometimes supposed me to mean, I ever wrote a line, even in fiction, contrary to my own profound beliefs. I have never said a thing I did not think: but I have sometimes had to abstain from saying many things I did think. When I wished to purvey strong meat for men, I was condemned to provide milk for babes. In the Hill-top Novels, I hope to reverse all that - to say my say in my own way, representing the world as it appears to me, not as editors and formalists would like me to represent it.

The Hill-top Novels, however, will not constitute, in the ordinary sense, a series. I shall add the name, as a Trade Mark, to any story, by whomsoever published, which I have written as the expression of my own individuality. Nor will they necessarily appear in the first instance in volume form. If ever I should be lucky enough to find an editor sufficiently bold and sufficiently righteous to venture upon running a Hill-top Novel as a serial through his columns, I will gladly embrace that mode of publication. But while editors remain as pusillanimous and as careless of moral progress as they are at present, I have little hope that I shall persuade any one of them to accept a work written with a single eye to the enlightenment and bettering of humanity.

Whenever, therefore, in future, the words "A Hill-top Novel" appear upon the title-page of a book by me, the reader who cares for truth and righteousness may take it for granted that the book represents my own original thinking, whether good or bad, on some important point in human society or human evolution.

Not, again, that any one of these novels will deliberately attempt to PROVE anything. I have been amused at the allegations brought by certain critics against The Woman who Did that it "failed to prove" the practicability of unions such as Herminia's and Alan's. The famous Scotsman, in the same spirit, objected to Paradise Lost that it "proved naething": but his criticism has not been generally endorsed as valid. To say the truth, it is absurd to suppose a work of imagination can prove or disprove anything. The author holds the strings of all his puppets, and can pull them as he likes, for good or evil: he can make his experiments turn out well or ill: he can contrive that his unions should end happily or miserably: how, then, can his story be said to PROVE anything? A novel is not a proposition in Euclid. I give due notice beforehand to reviewers in general, that if any principle at all is "proved" by any of my Hill-top Novels, it will be simply this: "Act as I think right, for the highest good of human kind, and you will infallibly and inevitably come to a bad end for it."

Not to prove anything, but to suggest ideas, to arouse emotions, is, I take it, the true function of fiction. One wishes to make one's readers THINK about problems they have never considered, FEEL with sentiments they have disliked or hated. The novelist as prophet has his duty defined for him in those divine words of Shelley's:

"Singing songs unbidden
Till the world is wrought
To sympathy with hopes and fears it heeded not."

That, too, is the reason that impels me to embody such views as these in romantic fiction, not in deliberate treatises. "Why sow your ideas broadcast," many honest critics say, "in novels where mere boys and girls can read them? Why not formulate them in serious and argumentative books, where wise men alone will come across them?" The answer is, because wise men are wise already: it is the boys and girls of a community who stand most in need of suggestion and instruction. Women, in particular, are the chief readers of fiction; and it is women whom one mainly desires to arouse to interest in profound problems by the aid of this vehicle. Especially should one arouse them to such living interest while they are still young and plastic, before they have crystallised and hardened into the conventional marionettes of polite society. Make them think while they are young: make them feel while they are sensitive: it is then alone that they will think and feel, if ever. I will venture, indeed, to enforce my views on this subject by a little apologue which I have somewhere read, or heard, - or invented.

A Revolutionist desired to issue an Election Address to the Working Men of Bermondsey. The Rector of the Parish saw it at the printer's, and came to him, much perturbed. "Why write it in English?" he asked. "It will only inflame the minds of the lower orders. Why not allow me to translate it into Ciceronian Latin? It would then be comprehensible to all University men; your logic would be duly and deliberately weighed: and the tanners and tinkers, who are so very impressionable, would not be poisoned by it." "My friend," said the Revolutionist, "it is the tanners and tinkers *I* want to get at. My object is, to win this election; University graduates will not help me to win it."

The business of the preacher is above all things to preach; but in order to preach, he must first reach his audience. The audience in this case consists in large part of women and girls, who are most simply and easily reached by fiction. Therefore, fiction is today the best medium for the preacher of righteousness who addresses humanity.

Why, once more, this particular name, "A Hill-top Novel"? For something like this reason.

I am writing in my study on a heather-clad hill-top. When I raise my eye from my sheet of foolscap, it falls upon miles and miles of broad open moorland. My window looks out upon unsullied nature. Everything around is fresh and pure and wholesome. Through the open casement, the scent of the pines blows in with the breeze from the neighbouring firwood. Keen airs sigh through the pine-needles. Grasshoppers chirp from deep tangles of bracken. The song of a skylark drops from the sky like soft rain in summer; in the evening, a nightjar croons to us his monotonously passionate love-wail from his perch on the gnarled boughs of the wind-swept larch that crowns the upland. But away below in the valley, as night draws on, a lurid glare reddens the north-eastern horizon. It marks the spot where the great wen of London heaves and festers. Up here on the free hills, the sharp air blows in upon us, limpid and clear from a thousand leagues of open ocean; down there in the crowded town, it stagnates and ferments, polluted with the diseases and vices of centuries.

This is an urban age. The men of the villages, alas, are leaving behind them the green fields and purple moors of their childhood, are foolishly crowding into the narrow lanes and purlieus of the great cities. Strange decadent sins and morbid pleasures entice them thither. But I desire in these books to utter a word once more in favour of higher and purer ideals of life and art. Those who sicken of the foul air and lurid light of towns may still wander side by side with me on these heathery highlands. Far, far below, the theatre and the music-hall spread their garish gas-lamps. Let who will heed them. But here on the open hill-top we know fresher and more wholesome delights. Those feverish joys allure us not. O decadents of the town, we have seen your sham idyls, your tinsel Arcadias. We have tired of their stuffy atmosphere, their dazzling jets, their weary ways, their gaudy dresses; we shun the sunken cheeks, the lack-lustre eyes, the heart-sick souls of your painted goddesses. We love not the fetid air, thick and hot with human breath, and reeking with tobacco smoke, of your modern Parnassus - a Parnassus whose crags were reared and shaped by the hands of the stage-carpenter! Your studied dalliance with your venal muses is little to our taste. Your halls are too stifling with carbonic acid gas; for us, we breathe oxygen.

And the oxygen of the hill-tops is purer, keener, rarer, more ethereal. It is rich in ozone. Now, ozone stands to common oxygen itself as the clean-cut metal to the dull and leaden exposed surface. Nascent and ever renascent, it has electrical attraction; it leaps to the embrace of the atom it selects, but only under the influence of powerful affinities; and what it clasps once, it clasps for ever. That is the pure air which we drink in on the heather-clad heights - not the venomous air of the crowded casino, nor even the close air of the middle-class parlour. It thrills and nerves us. How we smile, we who live here, when some dweller in the mists and smoke of the valley confounds our delicate atmosphere, redolent of honey and echoing the manifold murmur of bees, with that stifling miasma of the gambling hell and the dancing saloon! Trust me, dear friend, the moorland air is far other than you fancy. You can wander up here along the purple ridges, hand locked in hand with those you love, without fear of harm to yourself or your comrade. No Bloom of Ninon here, but fresh cheeks like the peach-blossom where the sun has kissed it: no casual fruition of loveless, joyless harlots, but life-long saturation of your own heart's desire in your own heart's innocence. Ozone is better than all the champagne in the Strand or Piccadilly. If only you will believe it, it is purity and life and sympathy and vigour. Its perfect freshness and perpetual fount of youth keep your age from withering. It crimsons the sunset and lives in the afterglow. If these delights thy mind may move, leave, oh, leave the meretricious town, and come to the airy peaks. Such joy is ours, unknown to the squalid village which spreads its swamps where the poet's silver Thames runs dull and leaden.

Have we never our doubts, though, up here on the hill-tops? Ay, marry, have we! Are we so sure that these gospels we preach with all our hearts are the true and final ones? Who shall answer that question? For myself, as I lift up my eyes from my paper once more, my gaze falls first on the golden bracken that waves joyously over the sandstone ridge without, and then, within, on a little white shelf where lies the greatest book of our greatest philosopher. I open it at random and consult its sortes. What comfort and counsel has Herbert Spencer for those who venture to see otherwise than the mass of their contemporaries?

"Whoever hesitates to utter that which he thinks the highest truth, lest it should be too much in advance of the time, may reassure himself by looking at his acts from an impersonal point of view. Let him duly realise the fact that opinion is the agency through which character adapts external arrangements to itself - that his opinion rightly forms part of this agency - is a unit of force, constituting, with other such units, the general power which works out social changes; and he will perceive that he may properly give full utterance to his innermost conviction; leaving it to produce what effect it may. It is not for nothing that he has in him these sympathies with some principles and repugnances to others. He, with all his capacities, and aspirations, and beliefs, is not an accident, but a product of the time. He must remember that while he is a descendant of the past, he is a parent of the future; and that his thoughts are as children born to him, which he may not carelessly let die. He, like every other man, may properly consider himself as one of the myriad agencies through whom works the Unknown Cause; and when the Unknown Cause produces in him a certain belief, he is thereby authorised to profess and act out that belief. For, to render in their highest sense the words of the poet -

> 'Nature is made better by no mean,
> But nature makes that mean; over that art
> Which you say adds to nature, is an art
> That nature makes.'

"Not as adventitious therefore will the wise man regard the faith which is in him. The highest truth he sees he will fearlessly utter; knowing that, let what may come of it, he is thus playing his right part in the world - knowing that if he can effect the change he aims at - well: if not - well also; though not SO well."

That passage comforts me. These, then, are my ideas. They may be right, they may be wrong. But at least they are the sincere and personal convictions of an honest man, warranted in him by that spirit of the age, of which each of us is but an automatic mouthpiece.

G. A.

I

The time was Saturday afternoon; the place was Surrey; the person of the drama was Philip Christy.

He had come down by the early fast train to Brackenhurst. All the world knows Brackenhurst, of course, the greenest and leafiest of our southern suburbs. It looked even prettier than its wont just then, that town of villas, in the first fresh tenderness of its wan spring foliage, the first full flush of lilac, laburnum, horse-chestnut, and guelder-rose. The air was heavy with the odour of May and the hum of bees. Philip paused a while at the corner, by the ivied cottage, admiring it silently. He was glad he lived there - so very aristocratic! What joy to glide direct, on the enchanted carpet of the South-Eastern Railway, from the gloom and din and bustle of Cannon Street, to the breadth and space and silence and exclusiveness of that upland village! For Philip Christy was a gentlemanly clerk in Her Majesty's Civil Service.

As he stood there admiring it all with roving eyes, he was startled after a moment by the sudden, and as it seemed to him unannounced apparition of a man in a well-made grey tweed suit, just a yard or two in front of him. He was aware of an intruder. To be sure, there was nothing very remarkable at first sight either in the stranger's dress, appearance, or manner. All that Philip noticed for himself in the newcomer's mien for the first few seconds was a certain distinct air of social superiority, an innate nobility of gait and bearing. So much at least he observed at a glance quite instinctively. But it was not this quiet and unobtrusive tone, as of the Best Society, that surprised and astonished him; Brackenhurst prided itself, indeed, on being a most well-bred and distinguished neighbourhood; people of note grew as thick there as heather or whortleberries. What puzzled him more was the abstruser question, where on earth the stranger could have come from so suddenly. Philip had glanced up the road and down the road just two minutes before, and was prepared to swear when he withdrew his eyes not a soul loomed in sight in either direction. Whence, then, could the man in the grey suit have emerged? Had he dropped from the clouds? No gate opened into the road on either side for two hundred yards or more; for Brackenhurst is one of those extremely respectable villa neighbourhoods where every house - an eligible family residence - stands in its own grounds of at least six acres. Now Philip could hardly suspect that so well dressed a man of such distinguished exterior would be guilty of such a gross breach of the recognised code of Brackenhurstian manners as was implied in the act of vaulting over a hedgerow. So he gazed in blank wonder at the suddenness of the apparition, more than half inclined to satisfy his curiosity by inquiring of the stranger how the dickens he had got there.

A moment's reflection, however, sufficed to save the ingenuous young man from the pitfall of so serious a social solecism. It would be fatal to accost him. For, mark you, no matter how gentlemanly and well-tailored a stranger may look, you can never be sure nowadays (in these topsy-turvy times of subversive radicalism) whether he is or is not really a gentleman. That makes acquaintanceship a dangerous luxury. If you begin by talking to a man, be it ever so casually, he may desire to thrust his company upon you, willy-nilly, in future; and when you have ladies of your family living in a place, you really CANNOT be too particular what companions you pick up there, were it even in the most informal and momentary fashion. Besides, the fellow might turn out to be one of your social superiors, and not care to know you; in which case, of course, you would only be letting yourself in for a needless snubbing. In fact, in this modern England of ours, this fatherland of snobdom, one passes one's life in a see-saw of doubt, between the Scylla and Charybdis of those two antithetical social dangers. You are always afraid you may get to know somebody you yourself do not want to know, or may try to know somebody who does not want to know you.

Guided by these truly British principles of ancestral wisdom, Philip Christy would probably never have seen anything more of the distinguished-looking stranger had it not been for a passing accident of muscular action, over which his control was distinctly precarious. He happened in brushing past to catch the stranger's eye. It was a clear blue eye, very deep and truthful. It somehow succeeded in riveting for a second Philip's attention. And it was plain the stranger was less afraid of speaking than Philip himself was. For he advanced with a pleasant smile on his open countenance, and waved one gloveless hand in a sort of impalpable or half- checked salute, which impressed his new acquaintance as a vaguely polite Continental gesture. This affected Philip favourably: the newcomer was a somebody then, and knew his place: for just in proportion as Philip felt afraid to begin conversation himself with an unplaced stranger, did he respect any other man who felt so perfectly sure of his own position that he shared no such middle-class doubts or misgivings. A duke is never afraid of accosting anybody. Philip was strengthened, therefore, in his first idea, that the man in the grey suit was a person of no small distinction in society, else surely he would not have come up and spoken with such engaging frankness and ease of manner.

"I beg your pardon," the stranger said, addressing him in pure and limpid English, which sounded to Philip like the dialect of the very best circles, yet with some nameless difference of intonation or accent which certainly was not foreign, still less provincial, or Scotch, or Irish; it seemed rather like the very purest well of English undefiled Philip had ever heard, - only, if anything, a little more so; "I beg your pardon, but I'm a stranger hereabouts, and I should be so VERY much obliged if you could kindly direct me to any good lodgings."

His voice and accent attracted Philip even more now he stood near at hand than his appearance had done from a little distance. It was impossible, indeed, to say definitely in set terms what there was about the man that made his personality and his words so charming; but from that very first minute, Philip freely admitted to himself that the stranger in the grey suit was a perfect gentleman. Nay, so much did he feel it in his ingenuous way that he threw off at once his accustomed cloak of dubious reserve, and, standing still to think, answered after a short pause, "Well, we've a great many very nice furnished houses about here to let, but not many lodgings. Brackenhurst's a cut above lodgings, don't you know; it's a residential quarter. But I should think Miss Blake's, at Heathercliff House, would perhaps be just the sort of thing to suit you."

"Oh, thank you," the stranger answered, with a deferential politeness which charmed Philip once more by its graceful expressiveness. "And could you kindly direct me to them? I don't know my way about at all, you see, as yet, in this country."

"With pleasure," Philip replied, quite delighted at the chance of solving the mystery of where the stranger had dropped from. "I'm going that way myself, and can take you past her door. It's only a few steps. Then you're a stranger in England?"

The newcomer smiled a curious self-restrained smile. He was both young and handsome. "Yes, I'm a stranger in your England," he answered, gravely, in the tone of one who wishes to avoid an awkward discussion. "In fact, an Alien. I only arrived here this very morning."

"From the Continent?" Philip inquired, arching his eyebrows slightly.

The stranger smiled again. "No, not from the Continent," he replied, with provoking evasiveness.

"I thought you weren't a foreigner," Philip continued in a blandly suggestive voice. "That is to say," he went on, after a second's pause, during which the stranger volunteered no further statement, "you speak English like an Englishman."

"Do I?" the stranger answered. "Well, I'm glad of that.

It'll make intercourse with your Englishmen so much more easy."

By this time Philip's curiosity was thoroughly whetted. "But you're not an Englishman, you say?" he asked, with a little natural hesitation.

"No, not exactly what you call an Englishman," the stranger replied, as if he didn't quite care for such clumsy attempts to examine his antecedents. "As I tell you, I'm an Alien. But we always spoke English at home," he added with an afterthought, as if ready to vouchsafe all the other information that lay in his power.

"You can't be an American, I'm sure," Philip went on, unabashed, his eagerness to solve the question at issue, once raised, getting the better for the moment of both reserve and politeness.

"No, I'm certainly not an American," the stranger answered with a gentle courtesy in his tone that made Philip feel ashamed of his rudeness in questioning him.

"Nor a Colonist?" Philip asked once more, unable to take the hint.

"Nor a Colonist either," the Alien replied curtly. And then he relapsed into a momentary silence which threw upon Philip the difficult task of continuing the conversation.

The member of Her Britannic Majesty's Civil Service would have given anything just that minute to say to him frankly, "Well, if you're not an Englishman, and you're not an American, and you're not a Colonist, and you ARE an Alien, and yet you talk English like a native, and have always talked it, why, what in the name of goodness do you want us to take you for?" But he restrained himself with difficulty. There was something about the stranger that made him feel by instinct it would be more a breach of etiquette to question him closely than to question any one he had ever met with.

They walked on along the road for some minutes together, the stranger admiring all the way the golden tresses of the laburnum and the rich perfume of the lilac, and talking much as he went of the quaintness and prettiness of the suburban houses. Philip thought them pretty, too (or rather, important), but failed to see for his own part where the quaintness came in. Nay, he took the imputation as rather a slur on so respectable a neighbourhood: for to be quaint is to be picturesque, and to be picturesque is to be old-fashioned. But the stranger's voice and manner were so pleasant, almost so ingratiating, that Philip did not care to differ from him on the abstract question of a qualifying epithet. After all, there's nothing positively insulting in calling a house quaint, though Philip would certainly have preferred, himself, to hear the Eligible Family Residences of that Aristocratic Neighbourhood described in auctioneering phrase as "imposing," "noble," "handsome," or "important-looking."

Just before they reached Miss Blake's door, the Alien paused for a second. He took out a loose handful of money, gold and silver together, from his trouser pocket. "One more question," he said, with that pleasant smile on his lips, "if you'll excuse my ignorance. Which of these coins is a pound, now, and which is a sovereign?"

"Why, a pound IS a sovereign, of course," Philip answered briskly, smiling the genuine British smile of unfeigned astonishment that anybody should be ignorant of a minor detail in the kind of life he had always lived among. To be sure, he would have asked himself with equal simplicity what was the difference between a twenty-franc piece, a napoleon, and a louis, or would have debated as to the precise numerical relation between twenty-five cents and a quarter of a dollar; but then, those are mere foreign coins, you see, which no fellow can be expected to understand, unless he happens to have lived in the country they are used in. The others are British and necessary to salvation. That feeling is instinctive in the thoroughly provincial English nature. No Englishman ever really grasps for himself the simple fact that England is a foreign country to foreigners; if strangers happen to show themselves ignorant of any petty matter in English life, he regards their ignorance as silly and childish, not to be compared for a moment to his own natural unfamiliarity with the absurd practices of foreign nations.

The Alien, indeed, seemed to have learned beforehand this curious peculiarity of the limited English intellect; for he blushed slightly as he replied, "I know your currency, as a matter of arithmetic, of course: twelve pence make one shilling; twenty shillings make one pound -"

"Of course," Philip echoed in a tone of perfect conviction; it would never have occurred to him to doubt for a moment that everybody knew intuitively those beggarly elements of the inspired British monetary system.

"Though they're singularly awkward units of value for any one accustomed to a decimal coinage: so unreasonable and illogical," the stranger continued blandly, turning over the various pieces with a dubious air of distrust and uncertainty.

"I BEG your pardon," Philip said, drawing himself up very stiff, and scarcely able to believe his ears (he was an official of Her Britannic Majesty's Government, and unused to such blasphemy). "Do I understand you to say, you consider pounds, shillings, and pence UNREASONABLE?"

He put an emphasis on the last word that might fairly have struck terror to the stranger's breast; but somehow it did not. "Why, yes," the Alien went on with imperturbable gentleness: "no order or principle, you know. No rational connection. A mere survival from barbaric use. A score, and a dozen. The score is one man, ten fingers and ten toes; the dozen is one man with shoes on - fingers and feet together. Twelve pence make one shilling; twenty shillings one pound. How very confusing! And then, the nomenclature's so absurdly difficult! Which of these is half-a-crown, if you please, and which is a florin? and what are their respective values in pence and shillings?"

Philip picked out the coins and explained them to him separately. The Alien meanwhile received the information with evident interest, as a traveller in that vast tract that is called Abroad might note the habits and manners of some savage tribe that dwells within its confines, and solemnly wrapped each coin up in paper, as his instructor named it for him, writing the designation and value outside in a peculiarly beautiful and legible hand. "It's so puzzling, you see," he said in explanation, as Philip smiled another superior and condescending British smile at this infantile proceeding; "the currency itself has no congruity or order: and then, even these queer unrelated coins haven't for the most part their values marked in words or figures upon them."

"Everybody knows what they are," Philip answered lightly. Though for a moment, taken aback by the novelty of the idea, he almost admitted in his own mind that to people who had the misfortune to be born foreigners, there WAS perhaps a slight initial difficulty in this unlettered system. But then, you cannot expect England to be regulated throughout for the benefit of foreigners! Though, to be sure, on the one occasion when Philip had visited the Rhine and Switzerland, he had grumbled most consumedly from Ostend to Grindelwald, at those very decimal coins which the stranger seemed to admire so much, and had wondered why the deuce Belgium, Germany, Holland, and Switzerland could not agree among themselves upon a uniform coinage; it would be so much more convenient to the British tourist. For the British tourist, of course, is NOT a foreigner.

On the door-step of Miss Blake's Furnished Apartments for Families and Gentlemen, the stranger stopped again. "One more question," he interposed in that same suave voice, "if I'm not trespassing too much on your time and patience. For what sort of term - by the day, month, year - does one usually take lodgings?"

"Why, by the week, of course," Philip answered, suppressing a broad smile of absolute surprise at the man's childish ignorance.

"And how much shall I have to pay?" the Alien went on quietly. "Have you any fixed rule about it?"

"Of course not," Philip answered, unable any longer to restrain his amusement (everything in England was "of course" to Philip). "You pay according to the sort of accommodation you require, the number of your rooms, and the nature of the neighbourhood."

"I see," the Alien replied, imperturbably polite, in spite of Philip's condescending manner. "And what do I pay per room in this latitude and longitude?"

For twenty seconds, Philip half suspected his new acquaintance of a desire to chaff him: but as at the same time the Alien drew from his pocket a sort of combined compass and chronometer which he gravely consulted for his geographical bearings, Philip came to the conclusion he must be either a seafaring man or an escaped lunatic. So he answered him to the point. "I should think," he said quietly, "as Miss Blake's are extremely respectable lodgings, in a first-rate quarter, and with a splendid view, you'll probably have to pay somewhere about three guineas."

"Three what?" the stranger interposed, with an inquiring glance at the little heap of coins he still held before him.

Philip misinterpreted his glance. "Perhaps that's too much for you," he suggested, looking severe; for if people cannot afford to pay for decent rooms, they have no right to invade an aristocratic suburb, and bespeak the attention of its regular residents.

"Oh, that's not it," the Alien put in, reading his tone

aright. "The money doesn't matter to me. As long as I can get a tidy room, with sun and air, I don't mind what I pay. It's the guinea I can't quite remember about for the moment. I looked it up, I know, in a dictionary at home; but I'm afraid I've forgotten it. Let me see; it's twenty-one pounds to the guinea, isn't it? Then I'm to pay about sixty-three pounds a week for my lodgings."

This was the right spirit. He said it so simply, so seriously, so innocently, that Philip was quite sure he really meant it. He was prepared, if necessary, to pay sixty odd pounds a week in rent. Now, a man like that is the proper kind of man for a respectable neighbourhood. He'll keep a good saddle-horse, join the club, and play billiards freely. Philip briefly explained to him the nature of his mistake, pointing out to him that a guinea was an imaginary coin, unrepresented in metal, but reckoned by prescription at twenty-one shillings. The stranger received the slight correction with such perfect nonchalance, that Philip at once conceived a high opinion of his wealth and solvency, and therefore of his respectability and moral character. It was clear that pounds and shillings were all one to him. Philip had been right, no doubt, in his first diagnosis of his queer acquaintance as a man of distinction. For wealth and distinction are practically synonyms in England for one and the same quality, possession of the wherewithal.

As they parted, the stranger spoke again, still more at sea. "And are there any special ceremonies to be gone through on taking up lodgings?" he asked quite gravely. "Any religious rites, I mean to say? Any poojah or so forth? That is," he went on, as Philip's smile broadened, "is there any taboo to be removed or appeased before I can take up my residence in the apartments?"

By this time Philip was really convinced he had to do with a madman - perhaps a dangerous lunatic. So he answered rather testily, "No, certainly not; how absurd! you must see that's ridiculous. You're in a civilised country, not among Australian savages. All you'll have to do is to take the rooms and pay for them. I'm sorry I can't be of any further use to you, but I'm pressed for time to-day. So now, good-morning."

As for the stranger, he turned up the path through the lodging-house garden with curious misgivings. His heart failed him. It was half-past three by mean solar time for that particular longitude. Then why had this young man said so briskly, "Good morning," at 3.30 P.M., as if on purpose to deceive him? Was he laying a trap? Was this some wile and guile of the English medicine-men?

II

Next day was (not unnaturally) Sunday. At half-past ten in the morning, according to his wont, Philip Christy was seated in the drawing-room at his sister's house, smooth silk hat in gloved hand, waiting for Frida and her husband, Robert Monteith, to go to church with him. As he sat there, twiddling his thumbs, or beating the devil's tattoo on the red Japanese table, the housemaid entered. "A gentleman to see you, sir," she said, handing Philip a card. The young man glanced at it curiously. A visitor to call at such an early hour! - and on Sunday morning too! How extremely odd! This was really most irregular!

So he looked down at the card with a certain vague sense of inarticulate disapproval. But he noticed at the same time it was finer and clearer and more delicately engraved than any other card he had ever yet come across. It bore in simple unobtrusive letters the unknown name, "Mr. Bertram Ingledew."

Though he had never heard it before, name and engraving both tended to mollify Philip's nascent dislike. "Show the gentleman in, Martha," he said in his most grandiose tone; and the gentleman entered.

Philip started at sight of him. It was his friend the Alien. Philip was quite surprised to see his madman of last night; and what was more disconcerting still, in the self-same grey tweed home-spun suit he had worn last evening. Now, nothing can be more gentlemanly, don't you know, than a grey home-spun, IN its proper place; but its proper place Philip Christy felt was certainly NOT in a respectable suburb on a Sunday morning.

"I beg your pardon," he said frigidly, rising from his seat with his sternest official air - the air he was wont to assume in the anteroom at the office when outsiders called and wished to interview his chief "on important public business." "To what may I owe the honour of this visit?" For he did not care to be hunted up in his sister's house at a moment's notice by a most casual acquaintance, whom he suspected of being an escaped lunatic.

Bertram Ingledew, for his part, however, advanced towards his companion of last night with the frank smile and easy bearing of a cultivated gentleman. He was blissfully unaware of the slight he was putting upon the respectability of Brackenhurst by appearing on Sunday in his grey tweed suit; so he only held out his hand as to an ordinary friend, with the simple words, "You were so extremely kind to me last night, Mr. Christy, that as I happen to know nobody here in England, I ventured to come round and ask your advice in unexpected circumstances that have since arisen."

When Bertram Ingledew looked at him, Philip once more relented. The man's eye was so captivating. To say the truth, there was something taking about the mysterious stranger - a curious air of unconscious superiority - so that, the moment he came near, Philip felt himself fascinated. He only answered, therefore, in as polite a tone as he could easily muster, "Why, how did you get to know my name, or to trace me to my sister's?"

"Oh, Miss Blake told me who you were and where you lived," Bertram replied most innocently: his tone was pure candour; "and when I went round to your lodgings just now, they explained that you were out, but that I should probably find you at Mrs. Monteith's; so of course I came on here."

Philip denied the applicability of that naive "of course" in his inmost soul: but it was no use being angry with Mr. Bertram Ingledew. So much he saw at once; the man was so simple-minded, so transparently natural, one could not be angry with him. One could only smile at him, a superior cynical London-bred smile, for an unsophisticated foreigner. So the Civil Servant asked with a condescending air, "Well, what's your difficulty? I'll see if peradventure I can help you out of it." For he reflected to himself in a flash that as Ingledew had apparently a good round sum in gold and notes in his pocket yesterday, he was not likely to come borrowing money this morning.

"It's like this, you see," the Alien answered with charming simplicity, "I haven't got any luggage."

"Not got any luggage!" Philip repeated, awestruck, letting his jaw fall short, and stroking his clean-shaven chin with one hand. He was more doubtful than ever now as to the man's sanity or respectability. If he was not a lunatic, then surely he must be this celebrated Perpignan murderer, whom everybody was talking about, and whom the French police were just then engaged in hunting down for extradition.

"No; I brought none with me on purpose," Mr. Ingledew replied, as innocently as ever. "I didn't feel quite sure about the ways, or the customs, or the taboos of England. So I had just this one suit of clothes made, after an English pattern of the present fashion, which I was lucky enough to secure from a collector at home; and I thought I'd buy everything else I wanted when I got to London. I brought nothing at all in the way of luggage with me."

"Not even brush and comb?" Philip interposed, horrified.

"Oh, yes, naturally, just the few things one always takes in a vade-mecum," Bertram Ingledew answered, with a gracefully deprecatory wave of the hand, which Philip thought pretty enough, but extremely foreign. "Beyond that, nothing. I felt it would be best, you see, to set oneself up in things of the country in the country itself. One's surer then of getting exactly what's worn in the society one mixes in."

For the first and only time, as he said those words, the stranger struck a chord that was familiar to Philip. "Oh, of course," the Civil Servant answered, with brisk acquiescence, "if you want to be really up to date in your dress, you must go to first-rate houses in London for everything. Nobody anywhere can cut like a good London tailor."

Bertram Ingledew bowed his head. It was the acquiescent bow of the utter outsider who gives no opinion at all on the subject under discussion, because he does not possess any. As he probably came, in spite of his disclaimer, from America or the colonies, which are belated places, toiling in vain far in the rear of

Bond Street, Philip thought this an exceedingly proper display of bashfulness, especially in a man who had only landed in England yesterday. But Bertram went on half-musingly. "And you had told me," he said, "I'm sure not meaning to mislead me, there were no formalities or taboos of any kind on entering into lodgings. However, I found, as soon as I'd arranged to take the rooms and pay four guineas a week for them, which was a guinea more than she asked me, Miss Blake would hardly let me come in at all unless I could at once produce my luggage." He looked comically puzzled. "I thought at first," he continued, gazing earnestly at Philip, "the good lady was afraid I wouldn't pay her what I'd agreed, and would go away and leave her in the lurch without a penny, - which was naturally a very painful imputation. But when I offered to let her have three weeks' rent in advance, I saw that wasn't all: there was a taboo as well; she couldn't let me in without luggage, she said, because it would imperil some luck or talisman to which she frequently alluded as the Respectability of her Lodgings. This Respectability seems a very great fetich. I was obliged at last, in order to ensure a night's lodging of any sort, to appease it by promising I'd go up to London by the first train to-day, and fetch down my luggage."

"Then you've things at Charing Cross, in the cloak-room perhaps?" Philip suggested, somewhat relieved; for he felt sure Bertram Ingledew must have told Miss Blake it was HE who had recommended him to Heathercliff House for furnished apartments.

"Oh, dear, no; nothing," Bertram responded cheerfully. "Not a sack to my back. I've only what I stand up in. And I called this morning just to ask as I passed if you could kindly direct me to an emporium in London where I could set myself up in all that's necessary."

"A WHAT?" Philip interposed, catching quick at the unfamiliar word with blank English astonishment, and more than ever convinced, in spite of denial, that the stranger was an American.

"An emporium," Bertram answered, in the most matter-of-fact voice: "a magazine, don't you know; a place where they supply things in return for money. I want to go up to London at once this morning and buy what I require there."

"Oh, A SHOP, you mean," Philip replied, putting on at once his most respectable British sabbatarian air. "I can tell you of the very best tailor in London, whose cut is perfect; a fine flower of tailors: but NOT to-day. You forget you're in England, and this is Sunday. On the Continent, it's different: but you'll find no decent shops here open to-day in town or country."

Bertram Ingledew drew one hand over his high white brow with a strangely puzzled air. "No more I will," he said slowly, like one who by degrees half recalls with an effort some forgotten fact from dim depths of his memory. "I ought to have remembered, of course. Why, I knew that, long ago. I read it in a book on the habits and manners of the English people. But somehow, one never recollects these taboo days, wherever one may be, till one's pulled up short by them in the course of one's travels. Now, what on earth am I to do? A box, it seems, is the Open, Sesame of the situation. Some mystic value is attached to it as a moral amulet. I don't believe that excellent Miss Blake would consent to take me in for a second night without the guarantee of a portmanteau to respectablise me."

We all have moments of weakness, even the most irreproachable Philistine among us; and as Bertram said those words in rather a piteous voice, it occurred to Philip Christy that the loan of a portmanteau would be a Christian act which might perhaps simplify matters for the handsome and engaging stranger. Besides, he was sure, after all - mystery or no mystery - Bertram Ingledew was Somebody. That nameless charm of dignity and distinction impressed him more and more the longer he talked with the Alien. "Well, I think, perhaps, I could help you," he hazarded after a moment, in a dubious tone; though to be sure, if he lent the portmanteau, it would be like cementing the friendship for good or for evil; which Philip, being a prudent young man, felt to be in some ways a trifle dangerous; for who borrows a portmanteau must needs bring it back again - which opens the door to endless contingencies. "I MIGHT be able -"

At that moment, their colloquy was suddenly interrupted by the entry of a lady who immediately riveted Bertram Ingledew's attention. She was tall and dark, a beautiful woman, of that riper and truer beauty in face and form that only declares itself as character develops. Her features were clear cut, rather delicate than regular; her eyes were large and lustrous; her lips not too thin, but rich and tempting; her brow was high, and surmounted by a luscious wealth of glossy black hair which Bertram never remembered to have seen equalled before for its silkiness of texture and its strange blue sheen, like a plate of steel, or the grass of the prairies. Gliding grace distinguished her when she walked. Her motion was equable. As once the sons of God saw the daughters of men that they were fair, and straightway coveted them, even so Bertram Ingledew looked on Frida Monteith, and saw at the first glance she was a woman to be desired, a soul high-throned, very calm and beautiful.

She stood there for a moment and faced him, half in doubt, in her flowing Oriental or Mauresque robe (for she dressed, as Philip would have said, "artistically"), waiting to be introduced the while, and taking good heed, as she waited, of the handsome stranger. As for Philip, he hesitated, not quite certain in his own mind on the point of etiquette - say rather of morals - whether one ought or ought not to introduce "the ladies of one's family" to a casual stranger picked up in the street, who confesses he has come on a visit to England without a letter of introduction or even that irreducible minimum of respectability - a portmanteau. Frida, however, had no such scruples. She saw the young man was good-looking and gentlemanly, and she turned to Philip with the hasty sort of glance that says as plainly as words could say it, "Now, then! introduce me."

Thus mutely exhorted, though with a visible effort, Philip murmured half inarticulately, in a stifled undertone, "My sister, Mrs. Monteith - Mr. Bertram Ingledew," and then trembled inwardly.

It was a surprise to Bertram that the beautiful woman with the soul in her eyes should turn out to be the sister of the very commonplace young man with the boiled-fish expression he had met by the corner; but he disguised his astonishment, and only interjected, as if it were the most natural remark in the world: "I'm pleased to meet you. What a lovely gown! and how admirably it becomes you!"

Philip opened his eyes aghast. But Frida glanced down

at the dress with a glance of approbation. The stranger's frankness, though quaint, was really refreshing.

"I'm so glad you like it," she said, taking the compliment with quiet dignity, as simply as it was intended. "It's all my own taste; I chose the stuff and designed the make of it. And I know who this is, Phil, without your troubling to tell me; it's the gentleman you met in the street last night, and were talking about at dinner."

"You're quite right," Philip answered, with a deprecating look (as who should say, aside, "I really couldn't help it"). "He - he's rather in a difficulty." And then he went on to explain in a few hurried words to Frida, with sundry shrugs and nods of profoundest import, that the supposed lunatic or murderer or foreigner or fool had gone to Miss Blake's without luggage of any sort; and that, "Perhaps" - very dubitatively - "a portmanteau or bag might help him out of his temporary difficulties."

"Why, of course," Frida cried impulsively, with prompt decision; "Robert's Gladstone bag and my little brown trunk would be the very things for him. I could lend them to him at once, if only we can get a Sunday cab to take them."

"NOT before service, surely," Philip interposed, scandalised. "If he were to take them now, you know, he'd meet all the church-people."

"Is it taboo, then, to face the clergy with a Gladstone bag?"

Bertram asked quite seriously, in that childlike tone of simple inquiry that Philip had noticed more than once before in him. "Your bonzes object to meet a man with luggage? They think it unlucky?"

Frida and Philip looked at one another with quick glances, and laughed.

"Well, it's not exactly tabooed," Frida answered gently; "and it's not so much the rector himself, you know, as the feelings of one's neighbours. This is a very respectable neighbourhood - oh, quite dreadfully respectable - and people in the houses about might make a talk of it if a cab drove away from the door as they were passing. I think, Phil, you're right. He'd better wait till the church-people are finished."

"Respectability seems to be a very great object of worship in your village," Bertram suggested in perfect good faith. "Is it a local cult, or is it general in England?"

Frida glanced at him, half puzzled. "Oh, I think it's pretty general," she answered, with a happy smile. "But perhaps the disease is a little more epidemic about here than elsewhere. It affects the suburbs: and my brother's got it just as badly as any one."

"As badly as any one!" Bertram repeated with a puzzled air. "Then you don't belong to that creed yourself? You don't bend the knee to this embodied abstraction? - it's your brother who worships her, I suppose, for the family?"

"Yes; he's more of a devotee than I am," Frida went on, quite frankly, but not a little surprised at so much freedom in a stranger. "Though we're all of us tarred with the same brush, no doubt. It's a catching complaint, I suppose, respectability."

Bertram gazed at her dubiously. A complaint, did she say? Was she serious or joking? He hardly understood her. But further discussion was cut short for the moment by Frida good-humouredly running upstairs to see after the Gladstone bag and brown portmanteau, into which she crammed a few useless books and other heavy things, to serve as make-weights for Miss Blake's injured feelings.

"You'd better wait a quarter of an hour after we go to church," she said, as the servant brought these necessaries into the room where Bertram and Philip were seated. "By that time nearly all the church-people will be safe in their seats; and Phil's conscience will be satisfied. You can tell Miss Blake you've brought a little of your luggage to do for to-day, and the rest will follow from town to-morrow morning."

"Oh, how very kind you are!" Bertram exclaimed, looking down at her gratefully. "I'm sure I don't know what I should ever have done in this crisis without you."

He said it with a warmth which was certainly unconventional. Frida coloured and looked embarrassed. There was no denying he was certainly a most strange and untrammelled person.

"And if I might venture on a hint," Philip put in, with a hasty glance at his companion's extremely unsabbatical costume, "it would be that you shouldn't try to go out much to-day in that suit you're wearing; it looks peculiar, don't you know, and might attract attention."

"Oh, is that a taboo too?" the stranger put in quickly, with an anxious air. "Now, that's awfully kind of you. But it's curious, as well; for two or three people passed my window last night, all Englishmen, as I judged, and all with suits almost exactly like this one - which was copied, as I told you, from an English model."

"Last night; oh, yes," Philip answered. "Last night was Saturday; that makes all the difference. The suit's right enough in its way, of course, - very neat and gentlemanly; but NOT for Sunday. You're expected on Sundays to put on a black coat and waistcoat, you know, like the ones I'm wearing."

Bertram's countenance fell. "And if I'm seen in the street like this," he asked, "will they do anything to me? Will the guardians of the peace - the police, I mean - arrest me?"

Frida laughed a bright little laugh of genuine amusement.

"Oh, dear, no," she said merrily; "it isn't an affair of police at all; not so serious as that: it's only a matter of respectability."

"I see," Bertram answered. "Respectability's a religious or popular, not an official or governmental, taboo. I quite understand you. But those are often the most dangerous sort. Will the people in the street, who adore Respectability, be likely to attack me or mob me for disrespect to their fetich?"

"Certainly not," Frida replied, flushing up. He seemed

to be carrying a joke too far. "This is a free country. Everybody wears and eats and drinks just what he pleases."

"Well, that's all very interesting to me," the Alien went on with a charming smile, that disarmed her indignation; "for I've come here on purpose to collect facts and notes about English taboos and similar observances. I'm Secretary of a Nomological Society at home, which is interested in pagodas, topes, and joss-houses; and I've been travelling in Africa and in the South Sea Islands for a long time past, working at materials for a History of Taboo, from its earliest beginnings in the savage stage to its fully developed European complexity; so of course all you say comes home to me greatly. Your taboos, I foresee, will prove a most valuable and illustrative study."

"I beg your pardon," Philip interposed stiffly, now put upon his mettle. "We have NO taboos at all in England. You're misled, no doubt, by a mere playful facon de parler, which society indulges in. England, you must remember, is a civilised country, and taboos are institutions that belong to the lowest and most degraded savages."

But Bertram Ingledew gazed at him in the blankest astonishment. "No taboos!" he exclaimed, taken aback. "Why, I've read of hundreds. Among nomological students, England has always been regarded with the greatest interest as the home and centre of the highest and most evolved taboo development. And you yourself," he added with a courteous little bow, "have already supplied me with quite half a dozen. But perhaps you call them by some other name among yourselves; though in origin and essence, of course, they're precisely the same as the other taboos I've been examining so long in Asia and Africa. However, I'm afraid I'm detaining you from the function of your joss-house. You wish, no doubt, to make your genuflexions in the Temple of Respectability."

And he reflected silently on the curious fact that the English give themselves by law fifty-two weekly holidays a year, and compel themselves by custom to waste them entirely in ceremonial observances.

III

On the way to church, the Monteiths sifted out their new acquaintance.

"Well, what do you make of him, Frida?" Philip asked, leaning back in his place, with a luxurious air, as soon as the carriage had turned the corner. "Lunatic or sharper?"

Frida gave an impatient gesture with her neatly gloved hand. "For my part," she answered without a second's hesitation, "I make him neither: I find him simply charming."

"That's because he praised your dress," Philip replied, looking wise. "Did ever you know anything so cool in your life? Was it ignorance, now, or insolence?"

"It was perfect simplicity and naturalness," Frida answered with confidence. "He looked at the dress, and admired it, and being transparently naif, he didn't see why he shouldn't say so. It wasn't at all rude, I thought - and it gave me pleasure."

"He certainly has in some ways charming manners," Philip went on more slowly. "He manages to impress one. If he's a madman, which I rather more than half suspect, it's at least a gentlemanly form of madness."

"His manners are more than merely charming," Frida answered, quite enthusiastic, for she had taken a great fancy at first sight to the mysterious stranger. "They've such absolute freedom. That's what strikes me most in them. They're like the best English aristocratic manners, without the insolence; or the freest American manners, without the roughness. He's extremely distinguished. And, oh, isn't he handsome!"

"He IS good-looking," Philip assented grudgingly. Philip owned a looking-glass, and was therefore accustomed to a very high standard of manly beauty.

As for Robert Monteith, he smiled the grim smile of the wholly unfascinated. He was a dour business man of Scotch descent, who had made his money in palm-oil in the City of London; and having married Frida as a remarkably fine woman, with a splendid figure, to preside at his table, he had very small sympathy with what he considered her high-flown fads and nonsensical fancies. He had seen but little of the stranger, too, having come in from his weekly stroll, or tour of inspection, round the garden and stables, just as they were on the very point of starting for St. Barnabas: and his opinion of the man was in no way enhanced by Frida's enthusiasm. "As far as I'm concerned," he said, with his slow Scotch drawl, inherited from his father (for though London-born and bred, he was still in all essentials a pure Caledonian) - "As far as I'm concerned, I haven't the slightest doubt but the man's a swindler. I wonder at you, Frida, that you should leave him alone in the house just now, with all that silver. I stepped round before I left, and warned Martha privately not to move from the hall till the fellow was gone, and to call up cook and James if he tried to get out of the house with any of our property.

But you never seemed to suspect him. And to supply him with a bag, too, to carry it all off in! Well, women are reckless! Hullo, there, policeman; - stop, Price, one moment; - I wish you'd keep an eye on my house this morning. There's a man in there I don't half like the look of. When he drives away in a cab that my boy's going to call for him, just see where he stops, and take care he hasn't got anything my servants don't know about."

In the drawing-room, meanwhile, Bertram Ingledew was reflecting, as he waited for the church people to clear away, how interesting these English clothes-taboos and day-taboos promised to prove, beside some similar customs he had met with or read of in his investigations elsewhere. He remembered how on a certain morning of the year the High Priest of the Zapotecs was obliged to get drunk, an act which on any other day in the calendar would have been regarded by all as a terrible sin in him. He reflected how in Guinea and Tonquin, at a particular period once a twelvemonth, nothing is considered wrong, and everything lawful, so that the worst crimes and misdemeanours go unnoticed and unpunished. He smiled to think how some days are tabooed in certain countries, so that whatever you do on them, were it only a game of tennis, is accounted wicked; while some days are periods of absolute licence, so that whatever you do on them, were it murder itself, becomes fit and holy. To him and his people at home, of course, it was the intrinsic character of the act itself that made it right or wrong, not the particular day or week or month on which one happened to do it. What was wicked in June was wicked still in October. But not so among the unreasoning devotees of taboo, in Africa or in England. There, what was right in May became wicked in September, and what was wrong on Sunday became harmless or even obligatory on Wednesday or Thursday. It was all very hard for a rational being to understand and explain: but he meant to fathom it, all the same, to the very bottom - to find out why, for example, in Uganda, whoever appears before the king must appear stark naked, while in England, whoever appears before the queen must wear a tailor's sword or a long silk train and a headdress of ostrich-feathers; why, in Morocco, when you enter a mosque, you must take off your shoes and catch a violent cold, in order to show your respect for Allah; while in Europe, on entering a similar religious building, you must uncover your head, no matter how draughty the place may be, since the deity who presides there appears to be indifferent to the danger of consumption or chest-diseases for his worshippers; why certain clothes or foods are prescribed in London or Paris for Sundays and Fridays, while certain others, just equally warm or digestible or the contrary, are perfectly lawful to all the world alike on Tuesdays and Saturdays. These were the curious questions he had come so far to investigate, for which the fakirs and dervishes of every land gave such fanciful reasons: and he saw he would have no difficulty in picking up abundant examples of his subject-matter everywhere in England. As the metropolis of taboo, it exhibited the phenomena in their highest evolution. The only thing that puzzled him was how Philip Christy, an Englishman born, and evidently a most devout observer of the manifold taboos and juggernauts of his country, should actually deny their very existence. It was one more proof to him of the extreme caution necessary in all anthropological investigations before accepting the evidence even of well-meaning natives on points of religious or social usage, which they are often quite childishly incapable of describing in rational terms to outside inquirers. They take their own manners and customs for granted, and they cannot see them in their true relations or compare them with the similar manners and customs of other nationalities.

IV

Whether Philip Christy liked it or not, the Monteiths and he were soon fairly committed to a tolerably close acquaintance with Bertram Ingledew. For, as chance would have it, on the Monday morning Bertram went up to town in the very same carriage with Philip and his brother-in-law, to set himself up in necessaries of life for a six or eight months' stay in England. When he returned that night to Brackenhurst with two large trunks, full of underclothing and so forth, he had to come round once more to the Monteiths, as Philip anticipated, to bring back the Gladstone bag and the brown portmanteau. He did it with so much graceful and gracious courtesy, and such manly gratitude for the favour done him, that he left still more deeply than ever on Frida's mind the impression of a gentleman. He had found out all the right shops to go to in London, he said; and he had ordered everything necessary to social salvation at the very best tailor's, so strictly in accordance with Philip's instructions that he thought he should now transgress no more the sumptuary rules in that matter made and established, as long as he remained in this realm of England. He had commanded a black cut-away coat, suitable for Sunday morning; and a curious garment called a frock-coat, buttoned tight over the chest, to be worn in the afternoon, especially in London; and a still quainter coat, made of shiny broadcloth, with strange tails behind, which was considered "respectable," after seven P.M., for a certain restricted class of citizens - those who paid a particular impost known as income-tax, as far as he could gather from what the tailor told him: though the classes who really did any good in the state, the working men and so forth, seemed exempted by general consent from wearing it. Their dress, indeed, he observed, was, strange to say, the least cared for and evidently the least costly of anybody's.

He admired the Monteith children so unaffectedly, too, telling them how pretty and how sweet-mannered they were to their very faces, that he quite won Frida's heart; though Robert did not like it. Robert had evidently some deep-seated superstition about the matter; for he sent Maimie, the eldest girl, out of the room at once; she was four years old; and he took little Archie, the two-year-old, on his knee, as if to guard him from some moral or social contagion. Then Bertram remembered how he had seen African mothers beat or pinch their children till they made them cry, to avert the evil omen, when he praised them to their faces; and he recollected, too, that most fetichistic races believe in Nemesis - that is to say, in jealous gods, who, if they see you love a child too much, or admire it too greatly, will take it from you or do it some grievous bodily harm, such as blinding it or maiming it, in order to pay you out for thinking yourself too fortunate. He did not doubt, therefore, but that in Scotland, which he knew by report to be a country exceptionally given over to terrible superstitions, the people still thought their sanguinary Calvinistic deity, fashioned by a race of stern John Knoxes in their own image, would do some harm to an over-praised child, "to wean them from it." He was glad to see, however, that Frida at least did not share this degrading and hateful belief, handed down from the most fiendish of savage conceptions. On the contrary, she seemed delighted that Bertram should pat little Maimie on the head, and praise her sunny smile and her lovely hair "just like her mother's."

To Philip, this was all a rather serious matter. He felt he was responsible for having introduced the mysterious Alien, however unwillingly, into the bosom of Robert Monteith's family. Now, Philip was not rich, and Frida was supposed to have "made a good match of it" - that is to say, she had married a man a great deal wealthier than her own upbringing. So Philip, after his kind, thought much of the Monteith connection. He lived in lodgings at Brackenhurst, at a highly inconvenient distance from town, so as to be near their house, and catch whatever rays of reflected glory might fall upon his head like a shadowy halo from their horses and carriages, their dinners and garden-parties. He did not like, therefore, to introduce into his sister's house anybody that Robert Monteith, that moneyed man of oil, in the West African trade, might consider an undesirable acquaintance. But as time wore on, and Bertram's new clothes came home from the tailor's, it began to strike the Civil Servant's mind that the mysterious Alien, though he excited much comment and conjecture in Brackenhurst, was accepted on the whole by local society as rather an acquisition to its ranks than otherwise. He was well off: he was well dressed: he had no trade or profession: and Brackenhurst, undermanned, hailed him as a godsend for afternoon teas and informal tennis-parties. That ineffable air of distinction as of one royal born, which Philip had noticed at once the first evening they met, seemed to strike and impress almost everybody who saw him. People felt he was mysterious, but at any rate he was Someone. And then he had been everywhere - except in Europe; and had seen everything - except their own society: and he talked agreeably when he was not on taboos: and in suburban towns, don't you know, an outsider who brings fresh blood into the field - who has anything to say we do not all know beforehand - is always welcome! So Brackenhurst accepted Bertram Ingledew before long, as an eccentric but interesting and romantic person.

Not that he stopped much in Brackenhurst itself. He went up to town every day almost as regularly as Robert Monteith and Philip Christy. He had things he wanted to observe there, he said, for the work he was engaged upon. And the work clearly occupied the best part of his energies. Every night he came down to Brackenhurst with his notebook crammed full of modern facts and illustrative instances. He worked most of all in the East End, he told Frida confidentially: there he could see best the remote results of certain painful English customs and usages he was anxious to study. Still, he often went west, too; for the West End taboos, though not in some cases so distressing as the East End ones, were at times much more curiously illustrative and ridiculous. He must master all branches of the subject alike. He spoke so seriously that after a time Frida, who was just at first inclined to laugh at his odd way of putting things, began to take it all in the end quite as seriously as he did. He felt more at home with her than with anybody else at Brackenhurst. She had sympathetic eyes; and he lived on sympathy. He came to her so often for help in his difficulties that she soon saw he really meant all he said, and was genuinely puzzled in a very queer way by many varied aspects of English society.

In time the two grew quite intimate together. But on one point Bertram would never give his new friend the slightest information; and that was the whereabouts of that mysterious "home" he so often referred to. Oddly enough, no one ever questioned him closely on the subject. A certain singular reserve of his, which alternated curiously with his perfect frankness, prevented them from trespassing so far on his individuality. People felt they must not. Somehow, when Bertram Ingledew let it once be felt he did not wish to be questioned on any particular point, even women managed to restrain their curiosity: and he would have been either a very bold or a very insensitive man who would have ventured to continue questioning him any further. So, though many people hazarded guesses as to where he had come from, nobody ever asked him the point-blank question: Who are you, if you please, and what do you want here?

The Alien went out a great deal with the Monteiths. Robert himself did not like the fellow, he said: one never quite knew what the deuce he was driving at; but Frida found him always more and more charming, - so full of information! - while Philip admitted he was excellent form, and such a capital tennis player! So whenever Philip had a day off in the country, they three went out in the fields together, and Frida at least thoroughly enjoyed and appreciated the freedom and freshness of the newcomer's conversation.

On one such day they went out, as it chanced, into the meadows that stretch up the hill behind Brackenhurst. Frida remembered it well afterwards. It was the day when an annual saturnalia of vulgar vice usurps and pollutes the open downs at Epsom. Bertram did not care to see it, he said - the rabble of a great town turned loose to desecrate the open face of nature - even regarded as a matter of popular custom; he had looked on at much the same orgies before in New Guinea and on the Zambesi, and they only depressed him: so he stopped at Brackenhurst, and went for a walk instead in the fresh summer meadows. Robert Monteith, for his part, had gone to the Derby - so they call that orgy - and Philip had meant to accompany him in the dogcart, but remained behind at the last moment to take care of Frida; for Frida, being a lady at heart, always shrank from the pollution of vulgar assemblies. As they walked together across the lush green fields, thick with campion and yellow-rattle, they came to a dense copse with a rustic gate, above which a threatening notice-board frowned them straight in the face, bearing the usual selfish and anti-social inscription, "Trespassers will be prosecuted."

"Let's go in here and pick orchids," Bertram suggested, leaning over the gate. "Just see how pretty they are! The scented white butterfly! It loves moist bogland. Now, Mrs. Monteith, wouldn't a few long sprays of that lovely thing look charming on your dinner-table?"

"But it's preserved," Philip interposed with an awestruck face. "You can't go in there: it's Sir Lionel Longden's, and he's awfully particular."

"Can't go in there? Oh, nonsense," Bertram answered, with a merry laugh, vaulting the gate like a practised athlete. "Mrs. Monteith can get over easily enough, I'm sure. She's as light as a fawn. May I help you over?" And he held one hand out.

"But it's private," Philip went on, in a somewhat horrified voice; "and the pheasants are sitting."

"Private? How can it be? There's nothing sown here. It's all wild wood; we can't do any damage. If it was growing crops, of course, one would walk through it not at all, or at least very carefully. But this is pure woodland. Are the pheasants tabooed, then? or why mayn't we go near them?"

"They're not tabooed, but they're preserved," Philip answered somewhat testily, making a delicate distinction without a difference, after the fashion dear to the official intellect. "This land belongs to Sir Lionel Longden, I tell you, and he chooses to lay it all down in pheasants. He bought it and paid for it, so he has a right, I suppose, to do as he likes with it."

"That's the funniest thing of all about these taboos," Bertram mused, as if half to himself. "The very people whom they injure and inconvenience the most, the people whom they hamper and cramp and debar, don't seem to object to them, but believe in them and are afraid of them. In Samoa, I remember, certain fruits and fish and animals and so forth were tabooed to the chiefs, and nobody else ever dared to eat them. They thought it was wrong, and said, if they did, some nameless evil would at once overtake them. These nameless terrors, these bodiless superstitions, are always the deepest. People fight hardest to preserve their bogeys. They fancy some appalling unknown dissolution would at once result from reasonable action. I tried one day to persuade a poor devil of a fellow in Samoa who'd caught one of these fish, and who was terribly hungry, that no harm would come to him if he cooked it and ate it. But he was too slavishly frightened to follow my advice; he said it was taboo to the god-descended chiefs: if a mortal man tasted it, he would die on the spot: so nothing on earth would induce him to try it. Though to be sure, even there, nobody ever went quite so far as to taboo the very soil of earth itself: everybody might till and hunt where he liked. It's only in Europe, where evolution goes furthest, that taboo has reached that last silly pitch of injustice and absurdity. Well, we're not afraid of the fetich, you and I, Mrs. Monteith. Jump up on the gate; I'll give you a hand over!" And he held out one strong arm as he spoke to aid her.

Frida had no such fanatical respect for the bogey of vested interests as her superstitious brother, so she mounted the gate gracefully - she was always graceful. Bertram took her small hand and jumped her down on the other side, while Philip, not liking to show himself less bold than a woman in this matter, climbed over it after her, though with no small misgivings. They strolled on into the wood, picking the pretty white orchids by the way as they went, for some little distance. The rich mould underfoot was thick with sweet woodruff and trailing loosestrife. Every now and again, as they stirred the lithe brambles that encroached upon the path, a pheasant rose from the ground with a loud whir-r-r before them. Philip felt most uneasy. "You'll have the keepers after you in a minute," he said, with a deprecating shrug. "This is just full nesting time. They're down upon anybody who disturbs the pheasants."

"But the pheasants can't BELONG to any one," Bertram cried, with a greatly amused face. "You may taboo the land - I understand that's done - but surely you can't taboo a wild bird that can fly as it likes from one piece of ground away into another."

Philip enlightened his ignorance by giving him

off-hand a brief and profoundly servile account of the English game-laws, interspersed with sundry anecdotes of poachers and poaching. Bertram listened with an interested but gravely disapproving face. "And do you mean to say," he asked at last "they send men to prison as criminals for catching or shooting hares and pheasants?"

"Why, certainly," Philip answered. "It's an offence against the law, and also a crime against the rights of property."

"Against the law, yes; but how on earth can it be a crime against the rights of property? Obviously the pheasant's the property of the man who happens to shoot it. How can it belong to him and also to the fellow who taboos the particular piece of ground it was snared on?"

"It doesn't belong to the man who shoots it at all," Philip answered, rather angrily. "It belongs to the man who owns the land, of course, and who chooses to preserve it."

"Oh, I see," Bertram replied. "Then you disregard the rights of property altogether, and only consider the privileges of taboo. As a principle, that's intelligible. One sees it's consistent. But how is it that you all allow these chiefs - landlords, don't you call them? - to taboo the soil and prevent you all from even walking over it? Don't you see that if you chose to combine in a body and insist upon the recognition of your natural rights, - if you determined to make the landlords give up their taboo, and cease from injustice, - they'd have to yield to you, and then you could exercise your native right of going where you pleased, and cultivate the land in common for the public benefit, instead of leaving it, as now, to be cultivated anyhow, or turned into waste for the benefit of the tabooers?"

"But it would be WRONG to take it from them," Philip cried, growing fiery red and half losing his temper, for he really believed it. "It would be sheer confiscation; the land's their own; they either bought it or inherited it from their fathers. If you were to begin taking it away, what guarantee would you have left for any of the rights of property generally?"

"You didn't recognise the rights of property of the fellow who killed the pheasant, though," Bertram interposed, laughing, and imperturbably good-humoured. "But that's always the way with these taboos, everywhere. They subsist just because the vast majority even of those who are obviously wronged and injured by them really believe in them. They think they're guaranteed by some divine prescription. The fetich guards them. In Polynesia, I recollect, some chiefs could taboo almost anything they liked, even a girl or a woman, or fruit and fish and animals and houses: and after the chief had once said, 'It is taboo,' everybody else was afraid to touch them. Of course, the fact that a chief or a landowner has bought and paid for a particular privilege or species of taboo, or has inherited it from his fathers, doesn't give him any better moral claim to it. The question is, 'Is the claim in itself right and reasonable?' For a wrong is only all the more a wrong for having been long and persistently exercised. The Central Africans say, 'This is my slave; I bought her and paid for her; I've a right, if I like, to kill her and eat her.' The king of Ibo, on the West Coast, had a hereditary right to offer up as a human sacrifice the first man he met every time he quitted his palace; and he was quite surprised audacious freethinkers should call the morality of his right in question. If you English were all in a body to see through this queer land-taboo, now, which drives your poor off the soil, and prevents you all from even walking at liberty over the surface of the waste in your own country, you could easily -"

"Oh, Lord, what shall we do!" Philip interposed in a voice of abject terror. "If here isn't Sir Lionel!"

And sure enough, right across the narrow path in front of them stood a short, fat, stumpy, unimpressive little man, with a very red face, and a Norfolk jacket, boiling over with anger.

"What are you people doing here?" he cried, undeterred by the presence of a lady, and speaking in the insolent, supercilious voice of the English landlord in defence of his pheasant preserves. "This is private property. You must have seen the notice at the gate, 'Trespassers will be prosecuted.'"

"Yes, we did see it," Bertram answered, with his unruffled smile; "and thinking it an uncalled-for piece of aggressive churlishness, both in form and substance, - why, we took the liberty to disregard it."

Sir Lionel glared at him. In that servile neighbourhood, almost entirely inhabited by the flunkeys of villadom, it was a complete novelty to him to be thus bearded in his den. He gasped with anger. "Do you mean to say," he gurgled out, growing purple to the neck, "you came in here deliberately to disturb my pheasants, and then brazen it out to my face like this, sir? Go back the way you came, or I'll call my keepers."

"No, I will NOT go back the way I came," Bertram responded deliberately, with perfect self-control, and with a side-glance at Frida. "Every human being has a natural right to walk across this copse, which is all waste ground, and has no crop sown in it. The pheasants can't be yours; they're common property. Besides, there's a lady. We mean to make our way across the copse at our leisure, picking flowers as we go, and come out into the road on the other side of the spinney. It's a universal right of which no country and no law can possibly deprive us."

Sir Lionel was livid with rage. Strange as it may appear to any reasoning mind, the man really believed he had a natural right to prevent people from crossing that strip of wood where his pheasants were sitting. His ancestors had assumed it from time immemorial, and by dint of never being questioned had come to regard the absurd usurpation as quite fair and proper. He placed himself straight across the narrow path, blocking it up with his short and stumpy figure. "Now look here, young man," he said, with all the insolence of his caste: "if you try to go on, I'll stand here in your way; and if you dare to touch me, it's a common assault, and, by George, you'll have to answer at law for the consequences."

Bertram Ingledew for his part was all sweet reasonableness. He raised one deprecating hand. "Now, before we come to open hostilities," he said in a gentle voice, with that unfailing smile of his, "let's talk the matter over like rational beings. Let's try to be logical. This copse is considered yours by the actual law of the country you live in: your tribe permits it to you: you're allowed to taboo it. Very well, then; I make all possible allowances for your strange hallucination.

You've been brought up to think you had some mystic and intangible claim to this corner of earth more than other people, your even Christians. That claim, of course, you can't logically defend; but failing arguments, you want to fight for it. Wouldn't it be more reasonable, now, to show you had some RIGHT or JUSTICE in the matter? I'm always reasonable: if you can convince me of the propriety and equity of your claim, I'll go back as you wish by the way I entered. If not - well, there's a lady here, and I'm bound, as a man, to help her safely over."

Sir Lionel almost choked. "I see what you are," he gasped out with difficulty. "I've heard this sort of rubbish more than once before. You're one of these damned land-nationalising radicals."

"On the contrary," Bertram answered, urbane as ever, with charming politeness of tone and manner: "I'm a born conservative. I'm tenacious to an almost foolishly sentimental degree of every old custom or practice or idea; unless, indeed, it's either wicked or silly - like most of your English ones."

He raised his hat, and made as if he would pass on. Now, nothing annoys an angry savage or an uneducated person so much as the perfect coolness of a civilised and cultivated man when he himself is boiling with indignation. He feels its superiority an affront on his barbarism. So, with a vulgar oath, Sir Lionel flung himself point-blank in the way. "Damn it all, no you won't, sir!" he cried. "I'll soon put a stop to all that, I can tell you. You shan't go on one step without committing an assault upon me." And he drew himself up, four-square, as if for battle.

"Oh, just as you like," Bertram answered coolly, never losing his temper. "I'm not afraid of taboos: I've seen too many of them." And he gazed at the fat little angry man with a gentle expression of mingled contempt and amusement.

For a minute, Frida thought they were really going to fight, and drew back in horror to await the contest. But such a warlike notion never entered the man of peace's head. He took a step backward for a second and calmly surveyed his antagonist with a critical scrutiny. Sir Lionel was short and stout and puffy; Bertram Ingledew was tall and strong and well-knit and athletic. After an instant's pause, during which the doughty baronet stood doubling his fat fists and glaring silent wrath at his lither opponent, Bertram made a sudden dart forward, seized the little stout man bodily in his stalwart arms, and lifting him like a baby, in spite of kicks and struggles, carried him a hundred paces to one side of the path, where he laid him down gingerly without unnecessary violence on a bed of young bracken. Then he returned quite calmly, as if nothing had happened, to Frida's side, with that quiet little smile on his unruffled countenance.

Frida had not quite approved of all this small episode, for she too believed in the righteousness of taboo, like most other Englishwomen, and devoutly accepted the common priestly doctrine, that the earth is the landlord's and the fulness thereof; but still, being a woman, and therefore an admirer of physical strength in men, she could not help applauding to herself the masterly way in which her squire had carried his antagonist captive. When he returned, she beamed upon him with friendly confidence. But Philip was very much frightened indeed.

"You'll have to pay for this, you know," he said. "This is a law-abiding land. He'll bring an action against you for assault and battery; and you'll get three months for it."

"I don't think so," Bertram answered, still placid and unruffled. "There were three of us who saw him; and it was a very ignominious position indeed for a person who sets up to be a great chief in the country. He won't like the little boys on his own estate to know the great Sir Lionel was lifted up against his will, carried about like a baby, and set down in a bracken-bed. Indeed, I was more than sorry to have to do such a thing to a man of his years; but you see he WOULD have it. It's the only way to deal with these tabooing chiefs. You must face them and be done with it. In the Caroline Islands, once, I had to do the same thing to a cazique who was going to cook and eat a very pretty young girl of his own retainers. He wouldn't listen to reason; the law was on his side; so, being happily NOT a law-abiding person myself, I took him up in my arms, and walked off with him bodily, and was obliged to drop him down into a very painful bed of stinging plants like nettles, so as to give myself time to escape with the girl clear out of his clutches. I regretted having to do it so roughly, of course; but there was no other way out of it."

As he spoke, for the first time it really came home to Frida's mind that Bertram Ingledew, standing there before her, regarded in very truth the Polynesian chief and Sir Lionel Longden as much about the same sort of unreasoning people - savages to be argued with and cajoled if possible; but if not, then to be treated with calm firmness and force, as an English officer on an exploring expedition might treat a wrathful Central

African kinglet. And in a dim sort of way, too, it began to strike her by degrees that the analogy was a true one, that Bertram Ingledew, among the Englishmen with whom she was accustomed to mix, was like a civilised being in the midst of barbarians, who feel and recognise but dimly and half-unconsciously his innate superiority.

By the time they had reached the gate on the other side of the hanger, Sir Lionel overtook them, boiling over with indignation.

"Your card, sir," he gasped out inarticulately to the calmly innocent Alien; "you must answer for all this. Your card, I say, instantly!"

Bertram looked at him with a fixed gaze. Sir Lionel, having had good proof of his antagonist's strength, kept his distance cautiously.

"Certainly NOT, my good friend," Bertram replied, in a firm tone. "Why should *I*, who am the injured and insulted party, assist YOU in identifying me? It was you who aggressed upon my free individuality. If you want to call in the aid of an unjust law to back up an unjust and irrational taboo, you must find out for yourself who I am, and where I come from. But I wouldn't advise you to do anything so foolish. Three of us here saw you in the ridiculous position into which by your obstinacy you compelled me to put you; and you wouldn't like to hear us recount it in public, with picturesque details, to your brother magistrates. Let me say one thing more to you," he added, after a pause, in that peculiarly soft and melodious voice of his. "Don't you think, on reflection - even if you're foolish enough and illogical enough really to believe in the sacredness of the taboo by virtue of which you try to exclude your fellow-tribesmen from their fair share of enjoyment of the soil of England - don't you think you might at any rate exercise your imaginary powers over the land you arrogate to yourself with a little more gentleness and common politeness? How petty and narrow it looks to use even an undoubted right, far more a tribal taboo, in a tyrannical and needlessly aggressive manner! How mean and small and low and churlish! The damage we did your land, as you call it - if we did any at all - was certainly not a ha'pennyworth. Was it consonant with your dignity as a chief in the tribe to get so hot and angry about so small a value? How grotesque to make so much fuss and noise about a matter of a ha'penny! We, who were the aggrieved parties, we, whom you attempted to debar by main force from the common human right to walk freely over earth wherever there's nothing sown or planted, and who were obliged to remove you as an obstacle out of our path, at some personal inconvenience" - (he glanced askance at his clothes, crumpled and soiled by Sir Lionel's unseemly resistance) - "WE didn't lose our tempers, or attempt to revile you. We were cool and collected. But a taboo must be on its very last legs when it requires the aid of terrifying notices at every corner in order to preserve it; and I think this of yours must be well on the way to abolition. Still, as I should like to part friends" - he drew a coin from his pocket, and held it out between his finger and thumb with a courteous bow towards Sir Lionel - "I gladly tender you a ha'penny in compensation for any supposed harm we may possibly have done your imaginary rights by walking through the wood here."

V

For a day or two after this notable encounter between tabooer and taboo-breaker, Philip moved about in a most uneasy state of mind. He lived in constant dread of receiving a summons as a party to an assault upon a most respectable and respected landed proprietor who preserved more pheasants and owned more ruinous cottages than anybody else (except the duke) round about Brackenhurst. Indeed, so deeply did he regret his involuntary part in this painful escapade that he never mentioned a word of it to Robert Monteith; nor did Frida either. To say the truth, husband and wife were seldom confidential one with the other. But, to Philip's surprise, Bertram's prediction came true; they never heard another word about the action for trespass or the threatened prosecution for assault and battery. Sir Lionel found out that the person who had committed the gross and unheard-of outrage of lifting an elderly and respectable English landowner like a baby in arms on his own estate, was a lodger at Brackenhurst, variously regarded by those who knew him best as an escaped lunatic, and as a foreign nobleman in disguise, fleeing for his life from a charge of complicity in a Nihilist conspiracy: he wisely came to the conclusion, therefore, that he would not be the first to divulge the story of his own ignominious defeat, unless he found that damned radical chap was going boasting around the countryside how he had balked Sir Lionel. And as nothing was further than boasting from Bertram Ingledew's gentle nature, and as Philip and Frida both held their peace for good reasons of their own, the baronet never attempted in any way to rake up the story of his grotesque disgrace on what he considered his own property. All he did was to double the number of keepers on the borders of his estate, and to give them strict notice that whoever could succeed in catching the "damned radical" in flagrante delicto, as trespasser or poacher, should receive most instant reward and promotion.

During the next few weeks, accordingly, nothing of importance happened, from the point of view of the Brackenhurst chronicler; though Bertram was constantly round at the Monteiths' garden for afternoon tea or a game of lawn-tennis. He was an excellent player; lawn-tennis was most popular "at home," he said, in that same mysterious and non-committing phrase he so often made use of. Only, he found the racquets and balls (very best London make) rather clumsy and awkward; he wished he had brought his own along with him when he came here. Philip noticed his style of service was particularly good, and even wondered at times he did not try to go in for the All England Championship. But Bertram surprised him by answering, with a quiet smile, that though it was an excellent amusement, he had too many other things to do with his time to make a serious pursuit of it.

One day towards the end of June, the strange young man had gone round to The Grange - that was the name of Frida's house - for his usual relaxation after a very tiring and distressing day in London, "on important business." The business, whatever it was, had evidently harrowed his feelings not a little, for he was sensitively organised. Frida was on the tennis-lawn. She met him with much lamentation over the unpleasant fact that she had just lost a sister-in-law whom she had never cared for.

"Well, but if you never cared for her," Bertram answered, looking hard into her lustrous eyes, "it doesn't much matter."

"Oh, I shall have to go into mourning all the same," Frida continued somewhat pettishly, "and waste all my nice new summer dresses. It's SUCH a nuisance!"

"Why do it, then?" Bertram suggested, watching her face very narrowly.

"Well, I suppose because of what you would call a fetich," Frida answered laughing. "I know it's ridiculous. But everybody expects it, and I'm not strong-minded enough to go against the current of what everybody expects of me."

"You will be by-and-by," Bertram answered, with confidence. "They're queer things, these death-taboos. Sometimes people cover their heads with filth or ashes; and sometimes they bedizen them with crape and white streamers. In some countries, the survivors are bound to shed so many tears, to measure, in memory of the departed; and if they can't bring them up naturally in sufficient quantities, they have to be beaten with rods, or pricked with thorns, or stung with nettles, till they've filled to the last drop the regulation bottle. In Swaziland, too, when the king dies, so the queen told me, every family of his subjects has to lose one of its sons or daughters, in order that they may all truly grieve at the loss of their sovereign. I think there are more horrible and cruel devices in the way of death-taboos and death-customs than anything else I've met in my researches. Indeed, most of our nomologists at home believe that all taboos originally arose out of ancestral ghost-worship, and sprang from the craven fear of dead kings or dead relatives. They think fetiches and gods and other imaginary supernatural beings were all in the last resort developed out of ghosts, hostile or friendly; and from what I see abroad, I incline to agree with them. But this mourning superstition, now - surely it must do a great deal of harm in poor households in England. People who can very ill afford to throw away good dresses must have to give them up, and get new black ones, and that often at the very moment when they're just deprived of the aid of their only support and bread-winner. I wonder it doesn't occur to them that this is absolutely wrong, and that they oughtn't to prefer the meaningless fetich to their clear moral duty."

"They're afraid of what people would say of them," Frida ventured to interpose. "You see, we're all so frightened of breaking through an established custom."

"Yes, I notice that always, wherever I go in England," Bertram answered. "There's apparently no clear idea of what's right and wrong at all, in the ethical sense, as apart from what's usual. I was talking to a lady up in London to-day about a certain matter I may perhaps mention to you by-and-by when occasion serves, and she said she'd been 'always brought up to think' so-and-so. It seemed to me a very queer substitute indeed for thinking."

"I never thought of that," Frida answered slowly. "I've said the same thing a hundred times over myself before now; and I see how irrational it is. But, there, Mr. Ingledew, that's why I always like talking with you so much: you make one take such a totally new view of things."

She looked down and was silent a minute. Her breast heaved and fell. She was a beautiful woman, very tall and queenly. Bertram looked at her and paused; then he went on hurriedly, just to break the awkward silence: "And this dance at Exeter, then - I suppose you won't go to it?"

"Oh, I CAN'T, of course," Frida answered quickly. "And my two other nieces - Robert's side, you know - who have nothing at all to do with my brother Tom's wife, out there in India - they'll be SO disappointed. I was going to take them down to it. Nasty thing! How annoying of her! She might have chosen some other time to go and die, I'm sure, than just when she knew I wanted to go to Exeter!"

"Well, if it would be any convenience to you," Bertram put in with a serious face, "I'm rather busy on Wednesday; but I could manage to take up a portmanteau to town with my dress things in the morning, meet the girls at Paddington, and run down by the evening express in time to go with them to the hotel you meant to stop at. They're those two pretty blondes I met here at tea last Sunday, aren't they?"

Frida looked at him, half-incredulous. He was very nice, she knew, and very quaint and fresh and unsophisticated and unconventional; but could he be really quite so ignorant of the common usages of civilised society as to suppose it possible he could run down alone with two young girls to stop by themselves, without even a chaperon, at an hotel at Exeter? She gazed at him curiously. "Oh, Mr. Ingledew," she said, "now you're really TOO ridiculous!"

Bertram coloured up like a boy. If she had been in any doubt before as to his sincerity and simplicity, she could be so no longer. "Oh, I forgot about the taboo," he said. "I'm so sorry I hurt you. I was only thinking what a pity those two nice girls should be cheated out of their expected pleasure by a silly question of pretended mourning, where even you yourself, who have got to wear it, don't assume that you feel the slightest tinge of sorrow. I remember now, of course, what a lady told me in London the other day: your young girls aren't even allowed to go out travelling alone without their mother or brothers, in order to taboo them absolutely beforehand for the possible husband who may some day marry them. It was a pitiful tale. I thought it all most painful and shocking."

"But you don't mean to say," Frida cried, equally shocked and astonished in her turn, "that you'd let young girls go out alone anywhere with unmarried men? Goodness gracious, how dreadful!"

"Why not?" Bertram asked, with transparent simplicity.

"Why, just consider the consequences!" Frida exclaimed, with a blush, after a moment's hesitation.

"There couldn't be ANY consequences, unless they both liked and respected one another," Bertram answered in the most matter-of-course voice in the world; "and if they do that, we think at home it's nobody's business to interfere in any way with the free expression of their individuality, in this the most sacred and personal matter of human intercourse. It's the one point of private conduct about which we're all at home most sensitively anxious not to meddle, to interfere, or even to criticise. We think such affairs should be left entirely to the hearts and consciences of the two persons concerned, who must surely know best how they feel towards one another. But I remember having met lots of taboos among other barbarians, in much the same way, to preserve the mere material purity of their women - a thing we at home wouldn't dream of even questioning. In New Ireland, for instance, I saw poor girls confined for four or five years in small wickerwork cages, where they're kept in the dark, and not even allowed to set foot on the ground on any pretext. They're shut up in these prisons when they're about fourteen, and there they're kept, strictly tabooed, till they're just going to be married. I went to see them myself; it was a horrid sight. The poor creatures were confined in a dark, close hut, without air or ventilation, in that stifling climate, which is as unendurable from heat as this one is from cold and damp and fogginess; and there they sat in cages, coarsely woven from broad leaves of the pandanus trees, so that no light could enter; for the people believed that light would kill them. No man might see them, because it was close taboo; but at last, with great difficulty, I persuaded the chief and the old lady who guarded them to let them come out for a minute to look at me. A lot of beads and cloth overcame these people's scruples; and with great reluctance they opened the cages. But only the old woman looked; the chief was afraid, and turned his head the other way, mumbling charms to his fetich. Out they stole, one by one, poor souls, ashamed and frightened, hiding their faces in their hands, thinking I was going to hurt them or eat them - just as your nieces would do if I proposed to-day to take them to Exeter - and a dreadful sight they were, cramped with long sitting in one close position, and their eyes all blinded by the glare of the sunlight after the long darkness. I've seen women shut up in pretty much the same way in other countries, but I never saw quite so bad a case as this of New Ireland."

"Well, you can't say we've anything answering to that in England," Frida put in, looking across at him with her frank, open countenance.

"No, not quite like that, in detail, perhaps, but pretty much the same in general principle," Bertram answered warmly. "Your girls here are not cooped up in actual cages, but they're confined in barrack-schools, as like prisons as possible; and they're repressed at every turn in every natural instinct of play or society. They mustn't go here or they mustn't go there; they mustn't talk to this one or to that one; they mustn't do this, or that, or the other; their whole life is bound round, I'm told, by a closely woven web of restrictions and restraints, which have no other object or end in view than the interests of a purely hypothetical husband. The Chinese cramp their women's feet to make them small and useless: you cramp your women's brains for the self-same purpose. Even light's excluded; for they mustn't read books that would make them think; they mustn't be allowed to suspect the bare possibility that the world may be otherwise than as their priests and nurses and grandmothers tell them, though most even of your own men know it well to be something quite different. Why, I met a girl at that dance I went to in London the other evening, who told me she wasn't allowed to read a book called Tess of the D'Urbervilles, that I'd read myself, and that seemed to me one of which every young girl and married woman in England ought to be given a copy. It was the one true book I had seen in your country. And another girl wasn't allowed to read another book, which I've since looked at, called Robert Elsmere, - an ephemeral thing enough in its way, I don't doubt, but proscribed in her case for no other reason on earth than because it expressed some mild disbelief as to the exact literary accuracy of those Lower Syrian pamphlets to which your priests attach such immense importance."

"Oh, Mr. Ingledew," Frida cried, trembling, yet profoundly interested; "if you talk like that any more, I shan't be able to listen to you."

"There it is, you see," Bertram continued, with a little wave of the hand. "You've been so blinded and bedimmed by being deprived of light when a girl, that now, when you see even a very faint ray, it dazzles you and frightens you. That mustn't be so - it needn't, I feel confident. I shall have to teach you how to bear the light. Your eyes, I know, are naturally strong; you were an eagle born: you'd soon get used to it."

Frida lifted them slowly, those beautiful eyes, and met his own with genuine pleasure.

"Do you think so?" she asked, half whispering. In some dim, instinctive way she felt this strange man was a superior being, and that every small crumb of praise from him was well worth meriting.

"Why, Frida, of course I do," he answered, without the least sense of impertinence. "Do you think if I didn't I'd have taken so much trouble to try and educate you?" For he had talked to her much in their walks on the hillside.

Frida did not correct him for his bold application of her Christian name, though she knew she ought to. She only looked up at him and answered gravely -

"I certainly can't let you take my nieces to Exeter."

"I suppose not," he replied, hardly catching at her meaning. "One of the girls at that dance the other night told me a great many queer facts about your taboos on these domestic subjects; so I know how stringent and how unreasoning they are. And, indeed, I found out a little bit for myself; for there was one nice girl there, to whom I took a very great fancy; and I was just going to kiss her as I said good-night, when she drew back suddenly, almost as if I'd struck her, though we'd been talking together quite confidentially a minute before. I could see she thought I really meant to insult her. Of course, I explained it was only what I'd have done to any nice girl at home under similar circumstances; but she didn't seem to believe me. And the oddest part of it all was, that all the time we were dancing I had my arm round her waist, as all the other men had theirs round their partners; and at home we consider it a much greater proof of confidence and affection to be allowed to place your arm round a lady's waist than merely to kiss her."

Frida felt the conversation was beginning to travel beyond her ideas of propriety, so she checked its excursions by answering gravely: "Oh, Mr. Ingledew, you don't understand our code of morals. But I'm sure you don't find your East End young ladies so fearfully particular?"

"They certainly haven't quite so many taboos," Bertram answered quietly. "But that's always the way in tabooing societies. These things are naturally worst among the chiefs and great people. I remember when I was stopping among the Ot Danoms of Borneo, the daughters of chiefs and great sun-descended families were shut up at eight or ten years old, in a little cell or room, as a religious duty, and cut off from all intercourse with the outside world for many years together. The cell's dimly lit by a single small window, placed high in the wall, so that the unhappy girl never sees anybody or anything, but passes her life in almost total darkness. She mayn't leave the room on any pretext whatever, not even for the most pressing and necessary purposes. None of her family may see her face; but a single slave woman's appointed to accompany her and wait upon her. Long want of exercise stunts her bodily growth, and when at last she becomes a woman, and emerges from her prison, her complexion has grown wan and pale and waxlike. They take her out in solemn guise and show her the sun, the sky, the land, the water, the trees, the flowers, and tell her all their names, as if to a newborn creature. Then a great feast is made, a poor crouching slave is killed with a blow of the sword, and the girl is solemnly smeared with his reeking blood, by way of initiation. But this is only done, of course, with the daughters of wealthy and powerful families. And I find it pretty much the same in England. In all these matters, your poorer classes are relatively pure and simple and natural. It's your richer and worse and more selfish classes among whom sex-taboos are strongest and most unnatural."

Frida looked up at him a little pleadingly.

"Do you know, Mr. Ingledew," she said, in a trembling voice, "I'm sure you don't mean it for intentional rudeness, but it sounds to us very like it, when you speak of our taboos and compare us openly to these dreadful savages. I'm a woman, I know; but - I don't like to hear you speak so about my England."

The words took Bertram fairly by surprise. He was wholly unacquainted with that rank form of provincialism which we know as patriotism. He leaned across towards her with a look of deep pain on his handsome face.

"Oh, Mrs. Monteith," he cried earnestly, "if YOU don't like it, I'll never again speak of them as taboos in your presence. I didn't dream you could object. It seems so natural to us - well - to describe like customs by like names in every case. But if it gives you pain - why, sooner than do that, I'd never again say a single word while I live about an English custom!"

His face was very near hers, and he was a son of Adam, like all the rest of us - not a being of another sphere, as Frida was sometimes half tempted to consider him. What might next have happened he himself hardly knew, for he was an impulsive creature, and Frida's rich lips were full and crimson, had not Philip's arrival with the two Miss Hardys to make up a set diverted for the moment the nascent possibility of a leading incident.

VI

It was a Sunday afternoon in full July, and a small party was seated under the spreading mulberry tree on the Monteiths' lawn. General Claviger was of the number, that well-known constructor of scientific frontiers in India or Africa; and so was Dean Chalmers, the popular preacher, who had come down for the day from his London house to deliver a sermon on behalf of the Society for Superseding the Existing Superstitions of China and Japan by the Dying Ones of Europe. Philip was there, too, enjoying himself thoroughly in the midst of such good company, and so was Robert Monteith, bleak and grim as usual, but deeply interested for the moment in dividing metaphysical and theological cobwebs with his friend the Dean, who as a brother Scotsman loved a good discussion better almost than he loved a good discourse. General Claviger, for his part, was congenially engaged in describing to Bertram his pet idea for a campaign against the Madhi and his men, in the interior of the Soudan. Bertram rather yawned through that technical talk; he was a man of peace, and schemes of organised bloodshed interested him no more than the details of a projected human sacrifice, given by a Central African chief with native gusto, would interest an average European gentleman. At last, however, the General happened to say casually, "I forget the exact name of the place I mean; I think it's

Malolo; but I have a very good map of all the district at my house down at Wanborough."

"What! Wanborough in Northamptonshire?" Bertram exclaimed with sudden interest. "Do you really live there?"

"I'm lord of the manor," General Claviger answered, with a little access of dignity. "The Clavigers or Clavigeros were a Spanish family of Andalusian origin, who settled down at Wanborough under Philip and Mary, and retained the manor, no doubt by conversion to the Protestant side, after the accession of Elizabeth."

"That's interesting to me," Bertram answered, with his frank and fearless truthfulness, "because my people came originally from Wanborough before - well, before they emigrated." (Philip, listening askance, pricked up his ears eagerly at the tell-tale phrase; after all, then, a colonist!) "But they weren't anybody distinguished - certainly not lords of the manor," he added hastily as the General turned a keen eye on him. "Are there any Ingledews living now in the Wanborough district? One likes, as a matter of scientific heredity, to know all one can about one's ancestors, and one's county, and one's collateral relatives."

"Well, there ARE some Ingledews just now at Wanborough," the General answered, with some natural hesitation, surveying the tall, handsome young man from head to foot, not without a faint touch of soldierly approbation; "but they can hardly be your relatives, however remote. . . . They're people in a most humble sphere of life. Unless, indeed - well, we know the vicissitudes of families - perhaps your ancestors and the Ingledews that I know drifted apart a long time ago."

"Is he a cobbler?" Bertram inquired, without a trace of mauvaise honte.

The General nodded. "Well, yes," he said politely, "that's exactly what he is; though, as you seemed to be asking about presumed relations, I didn't like to mention it."

"Oh, then, he's my ancestor," Bertram put in, quite pleased at the discovery. "That is to say," he added after a curious pause, "my ancestor's descendant. Almost all my people, a little way back, you see, were shoe-makers or cobblers."

He said it with dignity, exactly as he might have said they were dukes or lord chancellors; but Philip could not help pitying him, not so much for being descended from so mean a lot, as for being fool enough to acknowledge it on a gentleman's lawn at Brackenhurst. Why, with manners like his, if he had not given himself away, one might easily have taken him for a descendant of the Plantagenets.

So the General seemed to think too, for he added quickly, "But you're very like the duke, and the duke's a Bertram. Is he also a relative?"

The young man coloured slightly. "Ye-es," he answered, hesitating; "but we're not very proud of the Bertram connection. They never did much good in the world, the Bertrams. I bear the name, one may almost say by accident, because it was handed down to me by my grandfather Ingledew, who had Bertram blood, but was a vast deal a better man than any other member of the Bertram family."

"I'll be seeing the duke on Wednesday," the General put in, with marked politeness, "and I'll ask him, if you like, about your grandfather's relationship. Who was he exactly, and what was his connection with the present man or his predecessor?"

"Oh, don't, please," Bertram put in, half-pleadingly, it is true, but still with that same ineffable and indefinable air of a great gentleman that never for a moment deserted him. "The duke would never have heard of my ancestors, I'm sure, and I particularly don't want to be mixed up with the existing Bertrams in any way."

He was happily innocent and ignorant of the natural interpretation the others would put upon his reticence, after the true English manner; but still he was vaguely aware, from the silence that ensued for a moment after he ceased, that he must have broken once more some important taboo, or offended once more some much-revered fetich. To get rid of the awkwardness he turned quietly to Frida. "What do you say, Mrs. Monteith," he suggested, "to a game of tennis?"

As bad luck would have it, he had floundered from one taboo headlong into another. The Dean looked up, open-mouthed, with a sharp glance of inquiry. Did Mrs. Monteith, then, permit such frivolities on the Sunday? "You forget what day it is, I think," Frida interposed gently, with a look of warning.

Bertram took the hint at once. "So I did," he answered quickly. "At home, you see, we let no man judge us of days and of weeks, and of times and of seasons. It puzzles us so much. With us, what's wrong to-day can never be right and proper to-morrow."

"But surely," the Dean said, bristling up, "some day is set apart in every civilised land for religious exercises."

"Oh, no," Bertram replied, falling incautiously into the trap. "We do right every day of the week alike, - and never do poojah of any sort at any time."

"Then where do you come from?" the Dean asked severely, pouncing down upon him like a hawk. "I've always understood the very lowest savages have at least some outer form or shadow of religion."

"Yes, perhaps so; but we're not savages, either low or otherwise," Bertram answered cautiously, perceiving his error. "And as to your other point, for reasons of my own, I prefer for the present not to say where I come from. You wouldn't believe me, if I told you - as you didn't, I saw, about my remote connection with the Duke of East Anglia's family. And we're not accustomed, where I live, to be disbelieved or doubted. It's perhaps the one thing that really almost makes us lose our tempers. So, if you please, I won't go any further at present into the debatable matter of my place of origin."

He rose to stroll off into the gardens, having spoken all the time in that peculiarly grave and dignified tone that seemed natural to him whenever any one tried to question him closely. Nobody save a churchman would have continued the discussion. But the Dean was a churchman, and also a Scot, and he returned to the attack, unabashed and unbaffled. "But surely, Mr. Ingledew," he said in a persuasive voice, "your people, whoever they are, must at least acknowledge a creator of the universe."

Bertram gazed at him fixedly. His eye was stern. "My people, sir," he said slowly, in very measured words, unaware that one must not argue with a clergyman, "acknowledge and investigate every reality they can find in the universe - and admit no phantoms. They believe in everything that can be shown or proved to be natural and true; but in nothing supernatural, that is to say, imaginary or non-existent. They accept plain facts: they reject pure phantasies. How beautiful those lilies are, Mrs. Monteith! such an exquisite colour! Shall we go over and look at them?"

"Not just now," Frida answered, relieved at the appearance of Martha with the tray in the distance. "Here's tea coming." She was glad of the diversion, for she liked Bertram immensely, and she could not help noticing how hopelessly he had been floundering all that afternoon right into the very midst of what he himself would have called their taboos and joss-business.

But Bertram was not well out of his troubles yet. Martha brought the round tray - Oriental brass, finely chased with flowing Arabic inscriptions - and laid it down on the dainty little rustic table. Then she handed about the cups. Bertram rose to help her. "Mayn't I do it for you?" he said, as politely as he would have said it to a lady in her drawing-room.

"No, thank you, sir," Martha answered, turning red at the offer, but with the imperturbable solemnity of the well-trained English servant. She "knew her place," and resented the intrusion. But Bertram had his own notions of politeness, too, which were not to be lightly set aside for local class distinctions. He could not see a pretty girl handing cups to guests without instinctively rising from his seat to assist her. So, very much to Martha's embarrassment, he continued to give his help in passing the cake and the bread-and-butter. As soon as she was gone, he turned round to Philip. "That's a very pretty girl and a very nice girl," he said simply. "I wonder, now, as you haven't a wife, you've never thought of marrying her."

The remark fell like a thunderbolt on the assembled group. Even Frida was shocked. Your most open-minded woman begins to draw a line when you touch her class prejudices in the matter of marriage, especially with reference to her own relations. "Why, really, Mr. Ingledew," she said, looking up at him reproachfully, "you can't mean to say you think my brother could marry the parlour-maid!"

Bertram saw at a glance he had once more unwittingly run his head against one of the dearest of these strange people's taboos; but he made no retort openly. He only reflected in silence to himself how unnatural and how wrong they would all think it at home that a young man of Philip's age should remain nominally celibate; how horrified they would be at the abject misery and degradation such conduct on the part of half his caste must inevitably imply for thousands of innocent young girls of lower station, whose lives he now knew were remorselessly sacrificed in vile dens of tainted London to the supposed social necessity that young men of a certain class should marry late in a certain style, and "keep a wife in the way she's been accustomed to." He remembered with a checked sigh how infinitely superior they would all at home have considered that wholesome, capable, good-looking Martha to an empty-headed and useless young man like Philip; and he thought to himself how completely taboo had overlaid in these people's minds every ethical idea, how wholly it had obscured the prime necessities of healthy, vigorous, and moral manhood. He recollected the similar though less hideous taboos he had met with elsewhere: the castes of India, and the horrible pollution that would result from disregarding them; the vile Egyptian rule, by which the divine king, in order to keep up the so-called purity of his royal and god-descended blood, must marry his own sister, and so foully pollute with monstrous abortions the very stock he believed himself to be preserving intact from common or unclean influences. His mind ran back to the strange and complicated forbidden degrees of the Australian Blackfellows, who are divided into cross-classes, each of which must necessarily marry into a certain other, and into that other only, regardless of individual tastes or preferences. He remembered the profound belief of all these people that if they were to act in any other way than the one prescribed, some nameless misfortune or terrible evil would surely overtake them. Yet, nowhere, he thought to himself, had he seen any system which entailed in the end so much misery on both sexes, though more particularly on the women, as that system of closely tabooed marriage, founded upon a broad basis of prostitution and infanticide, which has reached its most appalling height of development in hypocritical and puritan England. The ghastly levity with which all Englishmen treated this most serious subject, and the fatal readiness with which even Frida herself seemed to acquiesce in the most inhuman slavery ever devised for women on the face of this earth, shocked and saddened Bertram's profoundly moral and sympathetic nature. He could sit there no longer to listen to their talk. He bethought him at once of the sickening sights he had seen the evening before in a London music-hall; of the corrupting mass of filth underneath, by which alone this abomination of iniquity could be kept externally decent, and this vile system of false celibacy whitened outwardly to the eye like Oriental sepulchres: and he strolled off by himself into the shrubbery, very heavy in heart, to hide his real feelings from the priest and the soldier, whose coarser-grained minds could never have understood the enthusiasm of humanity which inspired and informed him.

Frida rose and followed him, moved by some unconscious wave of instinctive sympathy. The four children of this world were left together on the lawn by the rustic table, to exchange views by themselves on the extraordinary behaviour and novel demeanour of the mysterious Alien.

VII

As soon as he was gone, a sigh of relief ran half-unawares through the little square party. They felt some unearthly presence had been removed from their midst. General Claviger turned to Monteith. "That's a curious sort of chap," he said slowly, in his military way. "Who is he, and where does he come from?"

"Ah, where does he come from? - that's just the question," Monteith answered, lighting a cigar, and puffing away dubiously. "Nobody knows. He's a mystery. He poses in the role. You'd better ask Philip; it was he who brought him here."

"I met him accidentally in the street," Philip answered, with an apologetic shrug, by no means well pleased at being thus held responsible for all the stranger's moral and social vagaries. "It's the merest chance acquaintance. I know nothing of his antecedents. I - er - I lent him a bag, and he's fastened himself upon me ever since like a leech, and come constantly to my sister's. But I haven't the remotest idea who he is or where he hails from. He keeps his business wrapped up from all of us in the profoundest mystery."

"He's a gentleman, anyhow," the General put in with military decisiveness. "How manly of him to acknowledge at once about the cobbler being probably a near relation! Most men, you know, Christy, would have tried to hide it; HE didn't for a second. He admitted his ancestors had all been cobblers till quite a recent period."

Philip was astonished at this verdict of the General's, for he himself, on the contrary, had noted with silent scorn that very remark as a piece of supreme and hopeless stupidity on Bertram's part. No fellow can help having a cobbler for a grandfather, of course: but he need not be such a fool as to volunteer any mention of the fact spontaneously.

"Yes, I thought it bold of him," Monteith answered, "almost bolder than was necessary; for he didn't seem to think we should be at all surprised at it."

The General mused to himself. "He's a fine soldierly fellow," he said, gazing after the tall retreating figure. "I should like to make a dragoon of him. He's the very man for a saddle. He'd dash across country in the face of heavy guns any day with the best of them."

"He rides well," Philip answered, "and has a wonderful seat. I saw him on that bay mare of Wilder's in town the other afternoon, and I must say he rode much more like a gentleman than a cobbler."

"Oh, he's a gentleman," the General repeated, with unshaken conviction: "a thoroughbred gentleman." And he scanned Philip up and down with his keen grey eye as if internally reflecting that Philip's own right to criticise and classify that particular species of humanity was a trifle doubtful. "I should much like to make a captain of hussars of him. He'd be splendid as a leader of irregular horse; the very man for a scrimmage!" For the General's one idea when he saw a fine specimen of our common race was the Zulu's or the Red Indian's - what an admirable person he would be to employ in killing and maiming his fellow-creatures!

"He'd be better engaged so," the Dean murmured reflectively, "than in diffusing these horrid revolutionary and atheistical doctrines." For the Church was as usual in accord with the sword; theoretically all peace, practically all bloodshed and rapine and aggression: and anything that was not his own opinion envisaged itself always to the Dean's crystallised mind as revolutionary and atheistic.

"He's very like the duke, though," General Claviger went on, after a moment's pause, during which everybody watched Bertram and Frida disappearing down the walk round a clump of syringas. "Very like the duke. And you saw he admitted some sort of relationship, though he didn't like to dwell upon it. You may be sure he's a by-blow of the family somehow. One of the Bertrams, perhaps the old duke who was out in the Crimea, may have formed an attachment for one of these Ingledew girls - the cobbler's sisters: I dare say they were no better in their conduct than they ought to be - and this may be the consequence."

"I'm afraid the old duke was a man of loose life and doubtful conversation," the Dean put in, with a tone of professional disapprobation for the inevitable transgressions of the great and the high-placed. "He didn't seem to set the example he ought to have done to his poorer brethren."

"Oh, he was a thorough old rip, the duke, if it comes to that," General Claviger responded, twirling his white moustache. "And so's the present man - a rip of the first water. They're a regular bad lot, the Bertrams, root and stock. They never set an example of anything to anybody - bar horse-breeding, - as far as I'm aware; and even at that their trainers have always fairly cheated 'em."

"The present duke's a most exemplary churchman," the Dean interposed, with Christian charity for a nobleman of position. "He gave us a couple of thousand last year for the cathedral restoration fund."

"And that would account," Philip put in, returning abruptly to the previous question, which had been exercising him meanwhile, "for the peculiarly distinguished air of birth and breeding this man has about him." For Philip respected a duke from the bottom of his heart, and cherished the common Britannic delusion that a man who has been elevated to that highest degree in our barbaric rank-system must acquire at the same time a nobler type of physique and countenance, exactly as a Jew changes his Semitic features for the European shape on conversion and baptism.

"Oh, dear, no," the General answered in his most decided voice. "The Bertrams were never much to look at in any way: and as for the old duke, he was as insignificant a little monster of red-haired ugliness as ever you'd see in a day's march anywhere. If he hadn't been a duke, with a rent-roll of forty odd thousand a year, he'd never have got that beautiful Lady Camilla to consent to marry him. But, bless you, women 'll do anything for the strawberry leaves. It isn't from the

Bertrams this man gets his good looks. It isn't from the Bertrams. Old Ingledew's daughters are pretty enough girls. If their aunts were like 'em, it's there your young friend got his air of distinction."

"We never know who's who nowadays," the Dean murmured softly. Being himself the son of a small Scotch tradesman, brought up in the Free Kirk, and elevated into his present exalted position by the early intervention of a Balliol scholarship and a studentship of Christ Church, he felt at liberty to moralise in such non-committing terms on the gradual decay of aristocratic exclusiveness.

"I don't see it much matters what a man's family was," the General said stoutly, "so long as he's a fine, well-made, soldierly fellow, like this Ingledew body, capable of fighting for his Queen and country. He's an Australian, I suppose. What tall chaps they do send home, to be sure! Those Australians are going to lick us all round the field presently."

"That's the curious part of it," Philip answered. "Nobody knows what he is. He doesn't even seem to be a British subject. He calls himself an Alien. And he speaks most disrespectfully at times - well, not exactly perhaps of the Queen in person, but at any rate of the monarchy."

"Utterly destitute of any feeling of respect for any power of any sort, human or divine," the Dean remarked, with clerical severity.

"For my part," Monteith interposed, knocking his ash off savagely, "I think the man's a swindler; and the more I see of him, the less I like him. He's never explained to us how he came here at all, or what the dickens he came for. He refuses to say where he lives or what's his nationality. He poses as a sort of unexplained Caspar Hauser. In my opinion, these mystery men are always impostors. He had no letters of introduction to anybody at Brackenhurst; and he thrust himself upon Philip in a most peculiar way; ever since which he's insisted upon coming to my house almost daily. I don't like him myself: it's Mrs. Monteith who insists upon having him here."

"He fascinates me," the General said frankly. "I don't at all wonder the women like him. As long as he was by, though I don't agree with one word he says, I couldn't help looking at him and listening to him intently."

"So he does me," Philip answered, since the General gave him the cue. "And I notice it's the same with people in the train. They always listen to him, though sometimes he preaches the most extravagant doctrines - oh, much worse than anything he's said here this afternoon. He's really quite eccentric."

"What sort of doctrines?" the Dean inquired, with languid zeal. "Not, I hope, irreligious?"

"Oh, dear, no," Philip answered; "not that so much. He troubles himself very little, I think, about religion. Social doctrines, don't you know; such very queer views - about women, and so forth."

"Indeed?" the Dean said quickly, drawing himself up very stiff: for you touch the ark of God for the modern cleric when you touch the question of the relations of the sexes. "And what does he say? It's highly undesirable men should go about the country inciting to rebellion on such fundamental points of moral order in public railway carriages." For it is a peculiarity of minds constituted like the Dean's (say, ninety-nine per cent. of the population) to hold that the more important a subject is to our general happiness, the less ought we all to think about it and discuss it.

"Why, he has very queer ideas," Philip went on, slightly hesitating; for he shared the common vulgar inability to phrase exposition of a certain class of subjects in any but the crudest and ugliest phraseology. "He seems to think, don't you know, the recognised forms of vice - well, what all young men do - you know what I mean - Of course it's not right, but still they do them -" The Dean nodded a cautious acquiescence. "He thinks they're horribly wrong and distressing; but he makes nothing at all of the virtue of decent girls and the peace of families."

"If I found a man preaching that sort of doctrine to my wife or my daughters," Monteith said savagely, "I know what *I*'d do - I'd put a bullet through him."

"And quite right, too," the General murmured approvingly.

Professional considerations made the Dean refrain from endorsing this open expression of murderous sentiment in its fullest form; a clergyman ought always to keep up some decent semblance of respect for the Gospel and the Ten Commandments - or, at least, the greater part of them. So he placed the tips of his fingers and thumbs together in the usual deliberative clerical way, gazed blankly through the gap, and answered with mild and perfunctory disapprobation:

"A bullet would perhaps be an unnecessarily severe form of punishment to mete out; but I confess I could excuse the man who was so far carried away by his righteous indignation as to duck the fellow in the nearest horse-pond."

"Well, I don't know about that," Philip replied, with an outburst of unwonted courage and originality; for he was beginning to like, and he had always from the first respected, Bertram. "There's something about the man that makes me feel - even when I differ from him most - that he believes it all, and is thoroughly in earnest. I dare say I'm wrong, but I always have a notion he's a better man than me, in spite of all his nonsense, - higher and clearer and differently constituted, - and that if only I could climb to just where he has got, perhaps I should see things in the same light that he does."

It was a wonderful speech for Philip - a speech above himself; but, all the same, by a fetch of inspiration he actually made it. Intercourse with Bertram had profoundly impressed his feeble nature. But the Dean shook his head.

"A very undesirable young man for you to see too much of, I'm sure, Mr. Christy," he said, with marked disapprobation. For, in the Dean's opinion, it was a most dangerous thing for a man to think, especially when he's young; thinking is, of course, so likely to unsettle him!

The General, on the other hand, nodded his stern grey head once or twice reflectively.

"He's a remarkable young fellow," he said, after a

pause; "a most remarkable young fellow. As I said before, he somehow fascinates me. I'd immensely like to put that young fellow into a smart hussar uniform, mount him on a good charger of the Punjaub breed, and send him helter-skelter, pull-devil, pull-baker, among my old friends the Duranis on the North-West frontier."

VIII

While the men talked thus, Bertram Ingledew's ears ought to have burned behind the bushes. But, to say the truth, he cared little for their conversation; for had he not turned aside down one of the retired gravel paths in the garden, alone with Frida?

"That's General Claviger of Herat, I suppose," he said in a low tone, as they retreated out of ear-shot beside the clump of syringas. "What a stern old man he is, to be sure, with what a stern old face! He looks like a person capable of doing or ordering all the strange things I've read of him in the papers."

"Oh, yes," Frida answered, misunderstanding for the moment her companion's meaning. "He's a very clever man, I believe, and a most distinguished officer."

Bertram smiled in spite of himself. "Oh, I didn't mean that," he cried, with the same odd gleam in his eyes Frida had so often noticed there. "I meant, he looked capable of doing or ordering all the horrible crimes he's credited with in history. You remember, it was he who was employed in massacring the poor savage Zulus in their last stand at bay, and in driving the Afghan women and children to die of cold and starvation on the mountain-tops after the taking of Kabul. A terrible fighter, indeed! A terrible history!"

"But I believe he's a very good man in private life," Frida put in apologetically, feeling compelled to say the best she could for her husband's guest. "I don't care for him much myself, to be sure, but Robert likes him. And he's awfully nice, every one says, to his wife and step-children."

"How CAN he be very good," Bertram answered in his gentlest voice, "if he hires himself out indiscriminately to kill or maim whoever he's told to, irrespective even of the rights and wrongs of the private or public quarrel he happens to be employed upon? It's an appalling thing to take a fellow-creature's life, even if you're quite, quite sure it's just and necessary; but fancy contracting to take anybody's and everybody's life you're told to, without any chance even of inquiring whether they may not be in the right after all, and your own particular king or people most unjust and cruel and blood-stained aggressors? Why, it's horrible to contemplate. Do you know, Mrs. Monteith," he went on, with his far-away air, "it's that that makes society here in England so difficult to me. It's so hard to mix on equal terms with your paid high priests and your hired slaughterers, and never display openly the feelings you entertain towards them. Fancy if you had to mix so yourself with the men who flogged women to death in Hungary, or with the governors and jailors of some Siberian prison! That's the worst of travel. When I was in Central Africa, I sometimes saw a poor black woman tortured or killed before my very eyes; and if I'd tried to interfere in her favour, to save or protect her, I'd only have got killed myself, and probably have made things all the worse in the end for her. And yet it's hard indeed to have to look on at, or listen to, such horrors as these without openly displaying one's disgust and disapprobation. Whenever

I meet your famous generals, or your judges and your bishops, I burn to tell them how their acts affect me; yet I'm obliged to refrain, because I know my words could do no good and might do harm, for they could only anger them. My sole hope of doing anything to mitigate the rigour of your cruel customs is to take as little notice of them as possible in any way whenever I find myself in unsympathetic society."

"Then you don't think ME unsympathetic?" Frida murmured, with a glow of pleasure.

"O Frida," the young man cried, bending forward and looking at her, "you know very well you're the only person here I care for in the least or have the slightest sympathy with."

Frida was pleased he should say so; he was so nice and gentle: but she felt constrained none the less to protest, for form's sake at least, against his calling her once more so familiarly by her Christian name. "NOT Frida to you, if you please, Mr. Ingledew," she said as stiffly as she could manage. "You know it isn't right. Mrs. Monteith, you must call me." But she wasn't as angry, somehow, at the liberty he had taken as she would have been in anybody else's case; he was so very peculiar.

Bertram Ingledew paused and checked himself.

"You think I do it on purpose," he said with an apologetic air; "I know you do, of course; but I assure you I don't. It's all pure forgetfulness. The fact is, nobody can possibly call to mind all the intricacies of your English and European customs at once, unless he's to the manner born, and carefully brought up to them from his earliest childhood, as all of you yourselves have been. He may recollect them after an effort when he thinks of them seriously; but he can't possibly bear them all in mind at once every hour of the day and night by a pure tour de force of mental concentration. You know it's the same with your people in other barbarous countries. Your own travellers say it themselves about the customs of Islam. They can't learn them and remember them all at every moment of their lives, as the Mohammedans do; and to make one slip there is instant death to them."

Frida looked at him earnestly. "But I hope," she said with an air of deprecation, pulling a rose to pieces, petal by petal, nervously, as she spoke, "you don't put us on quite the same level as Mohammedans. We're so much more civilised. So much better in every way. Do you know, Mr. Ingledew," and she hesitated for a minute, "I can't bear to differ from you or blame you in anything, because you always appear to me so wise and good and kind-hearted and reasonable; but it often surprises me, and even hurts me, when you seem to talk of us all as if we were just so many savages. You're always speaking about taboo, and castes, and poojah, and fetiches, as if we weren't civilised people at all, but utter barbarians. Now, don't you think - don't you admit, yourself, it's a wee bit unreasonable, or at any rate impolite, of you?"

Bertram drew back with a really pained expression on his handsome features. "O Mrs. Monteith!" he cried, "Frida, I'm so sorry if I've seemed rude to you! It's all the same thing - pure human inadvertence; inability to throw myself into so unfamiliar an attitude. I forget every minute that YOU do not recognise the essential identity of your own taboos and poojahs and fetiches with the similar and often indistinguishable taboos and poojahs and fetiches of savages generally. They all come from the same source, and often retain to the end, as in your temple superstitions and your marriage superstitions, the original features of their savage beginnings. And as to your being comparatively civilised, I grant you that at once; only it doesn't necessarily make you one bit more rational - certainly not one bit more humane, or moral, or brotherly in your actions."

"I don't understand you," Frida cried, astonished. "But there! I often don't understand you; only I know, when you've explained things, I shall see how right you are."

Bertram smiled a quiet smile.

"You're certainly an apt pupil," he said, with brotherly gentleness, pulling a flower as he went and slipping it softly into her bosom. "Why, what I mean's just this. Civilisation, after all, in the stage in which you possess it, is only the ability to live together in great organised communities. It doesn't necessarily imply any higher moral status or any greater rationality than those of the savage. All it implies is greater cohesion, more unity, higher division of functions. But the functions themselves, like those of your priests and judges and soldiers, may be as barbaric and cruel, or as irrational and unintelligent, as any that exist among the most primitive peoples. Advance in civilisation doesn't necessarily involve either advance in real knowledge of one's relations to the universe, or advance in moral goodness and personal culture. Some highly civilised nations of historic times have been more cruel and barbarous than many quite uncultivated ones. For example, the Romans, at the height of their civilisation, went mad drunk with blood at their gladiatorial shows; the Athenians of the age of Pericles and Socrates offered up human sacrifices at the Thargelia, like the veriest savages; and the Phoenicians and Carthaginians, the most civilised commercial people of the world in their time, as the English are now, gave their own children to be burnt alive as victims to Baal. The Mexicans were far more civilised than the ordinary North American Indians of their own day, and even in some respects than the Spanish Christians who conquered, converted, enslaved, and tortured them; but the Mexican religion was full of such horrors as I could hardly even name to you. It was based entirely on cannibalism, as yours is on Mammon. Human sacrifices were common - commoner even than in modern England, I fancy. New-born babies were killed by the priests when the corn was sown; children when it had sprouted; men when it was full grown; and very old people when it was fully ripe."

"How horrible!" Frida exclaimed.

"Yes, horrible," Bertram answered; "like your own worst customs. It didn't show either gentleness or rationality, you'll admit; but it showed what's the one thing essential to civilisation - great coherence, high organisation, much division of function. Some of the rites these civilised Mexicans performed would have made the blood of kindly savages run cold with horror. They sacrificed a man at the harvest festival by crushing him like the corn between two big flat stones. Sometimes the priests skinned their victim alive, and wore his raw skin as a mask or covering, and danced hideous dances, so disguised, in honour of the hateful deities whom their fancies had created - deities even more hateful and cruel, perhaps, than the worst of your own Christian Calvinistic fancies. I can't see, myself, that civilised people are one whit the better in all these respects than the uncivilised barbarian. They pull together better, that's all; but war, bloodshed, superstition, fetich-worship, religious rites, castes, class distinctions, sex taboos, restrictions on freedom of thought, on freedom of action, on freedom of speech, on freedom of knowledge, are just as common in their midst as among the utterly uncivilised."

"Then what you yourself aim at," Frida said, looking hard at him, for he spoke very earnestly - "what you yourself aim at is -?"

Bertram's eyes came back to solid earth with a bound.

"Oh, what we at home aim at," he said, smiling that sweet, soft smile of his that so captivated Frida, "is not mere civilisation (though, of course, we value that too, in its meet degree, because without civilisation and co-operation no great thing is possible), but rationality and tenderness. We think reason the first good - to recognise truly your own place in the universe; to hold your head up like a man, before the face of high heaven, afraid of no ghosts or fetiches or phantoms; to understand that wise and right and unselfish actions are the great requisites in life, not the service of non-existent and misshapen creatures of the human imagination. Knowledge of facts, knowledge of nature, knowledge of the true aspects of the world we live in, - these seem to us of first importance. After that, we prize next reasonable and reasoning goodness; for mere rule-of-thumb goodness, which comes by rote, and might so easily degenerate into formalism or superstition, has no honour among us, but rather the contrary. If any one were to say with us (after he had passed his first infancy) that he always did such and such a thing because he had been told it was right by his parents or teachers - still more because priests or fetich-men had commanded it - he would be regarded, not as virtuous, but as feeble or wicked - a sort of moral idiot, unable to distinguish rationally for himself between good and evil. That's not the sort of conduct WE consider right or befitting the dignity of a grown man or woman, an ethical unit in an enlightened community. Rather is it their prime duty to question all things, to accept no rule of conduct or morals as sure till they have thoroughly tested it."

"Mr. Ingledew," Frida exclaimed, "do you know, when you talk like that, I always long to ask you where on earth you come from, and who are these your people you so often speak about. A blessed people: I would like to learn about them; and yet I'm afraid to. You almost seem to me like a being from another planet."

The young man laughed a quiet little laugh of deprecation, and sat down on the garden bench beside the yellow rose-bush.

"Oh, dear, no, Frida," he said, with that transparent glance of his. "Now, don't look so vexed; I shall call you Frida if I choose; it's your name, and I like you. Why let this funny taboo of one's own real name stand in the way of reasonable friendship? In many savage countries a woman's never allowed to call her husband by his name, or even to know it, or, for the matter of that, to see him in the daylight. In your England, the arrangement's exactly reversed: no man's allowed to call a woman by her real name unless she's tabooed for life to him - what you Europeans call married to him. But let that pass. If one went on pulling oneself up short at every one of your customs, one'd never get any further in any question one was discussing. Now, don't be deceived by nonsensical talk about living beings in other planets. There are no such creatures. It's a pure delusion of the ordinary egotistical human pattern. When people chatter about life in other worlds, they don't mean life - which, of a sort, there may be there: - they mean human life - a very different and much less important matter. Well, how could there possibly be human beings, or anything like them, in other stars or planets? The conditions are too complex, too peculiar, too exclusively mundane. We are things of this world, and of this world only. Don't let's magnify our importance: we're not the whole universe. Our race is essentially a development from a particular type of monkey-like animal - the Andropithecus of the Upper Uganda eocene. This monkey-like animal itself, again, is the product of special antecedent causes, filling a particular place in a particular tertiary fauna and flora, and impossible even in the fauna and flora of our own earth and our own tropics before the evolution of those succulent fruits and grain-like seeds, for feeding on which it was specially adapted. Without edible fruits, in short, there could be no monkey; and without monkeys there could be no man."

"But mayn't there be edible fruits in the other planets?" Frida inquired, half-timidly, more to bring out this novel aspect of Bertram's knowledge than really to argue with him; for she dearly loved to hear his views of things, they were so fresh and unconventional.

"Edible fruits? Yes, possibly; and animals or something more or less like animals to feed upon them. But even if there are such, which planetoscopists doubt, they must be very different creatures in form and function from any we know on this one small world of ours. For just consider, Frida, what we mean by life. We mean a set of simultaneous and consecutive changes going on in a complex mass of organised carbon compounds. When most people say 'life,' however, - especially here with you, where education is undeveloped - they aren't thinking of life in general at all (which is mainly vegetable), but only of animal and often indeed of human life. Well, then, consider, even on this planet itself, how special are the conditions that make life possible. There must be water in some form, for there's no life in the desert. There must be heat up to a certain point, and not above or below it, for fire kills, and there's no life at the poles (as among Alpine glaciers), or what little there is depends upon the intervention of other life wafted from elsewhere - from the lands or seas, in fact, where it can really originate. In order to have life at all, as WE know it at least (and I can't say whether anything else could be fairly called life by any true analogy, until I've seen and examined it), you must have carbon, and oxygen, and hydrogen, and nitrogen, and many other things, under certain fixed conditions; you must have liquid water, not steam or ice: you must have a certain restricted range of temperature, neither very much higher nor very much lower than the average of the tropics. Now, look, even with all these conditions fulfilled, how diverse is life on this earth itself, the one place we really know - varying as much as from the oak to the cuttle-fish, from the palm to the tiger, from man to the fern, the sea-weed, or the jelly-speck. Every one of these creatures is a complex result of very complex conditions, among which you must never forget to reckon the previous existence and interaction of all the antecedent ones. Is it probable, then, even a priori, that if life or anything like it exists on any other planet, it would exist in forms at all as near our own as a buttercup is to a human being, or a sea-anemone is to a cat or a pine-tree?"

"Well, it doesn't look likely, now you come to put it so," Frida answered thoughtfully: for, though English, she was not wholly impervious to logic.

"Likely? Of course not," Bertram went on with conviction. "Planetoscopists are agreed upon it. And above all, why should one suppose the living organisms or their analogues, if any such there are, in the planets or fixed stars, possess any such purely human and animal faculties as thought and reason? That's just like our common human narrowness. If we were oaks, I suppose, we would only interest ourselves in the question whether acorns existed in Mars and Saturn." He paused a moment; then he added in an afterthought: "No, Frida; you may be sure all human beings, you and I alike, and thousands of others a great deal more different, are essential products of this one wee planet, and of particular times and circumstances in its history. We differ only as birth and circumstances have made us differ. There IS a mystery about who I am, and where I come from; I won't deny it: but it isn't by any means so strange or so marvellous a mystery as you seem to imagine. One of your own old sacred books says (as I remember hearing in the joss-house I attended one day in London), 'God hath made of one blood all the nations of the earth.' If for GOD in that passage we substitute COMMON DESCENT, it's perfectly true. We are all of one race; and I confess, when I talk to you, every day I feel our unity more and more profoundly." He bent over on the bench and took her tremulous hand. "Frida," he said, looking deep into her speaking dark eyes, "don't you yourself feel it?"

He was so strange, so simple-minded, so different in every way from all other men, that for a moment Frida almost half-forgot to be angry with him. In point of fact, in her heart, she was not angry at all; she liked to feel the soft pressure of his strong man's hand on her dainty fingers; she liked to feel the gentle way he was stroking her smooth arm with that delicate white palm of his. It gave her a certain immediate and unthinking pleasure to sit still by his side and know he was full of her. Then suddenly, with a start, she remembered her duty: she was a married woman, and she OUGHT NOT to do it. Quickly, with a startled air, she withdrew her hand. Bertram gazed down at her for a second, half taken aback by her hurried withdrawal.

"Then you don't like me!" he cried, in a pained tone; "after all, you don't like me!" One moment later, a ray of recognition broke slowly over his face. "Oh, I forgot," he said, leaning away. "I didn't mean to annoy you. A year or two ago, of course, I might have held your hand in mine as long as ever I liked. You were still a free being. But what was right then is wrong now, according to the kaleidoscopic etiquette of your countrywomen. I forgot all that in the heat of the moment. I recollected only we were two human beings, of the same race and blood, with hearts that beat and hands that lay together. I remember now, you must hide and stifle your native impulses in future: you're tabooed for life to Robert Monteith: I must needs respect his seal set upon you!"

And he drew a deep sigh of enforced resignation.

Frida sighed in return. "These problems are so hard,"

she said.

Bertram smiled a strange smile. "There are NO problems," he answered confidently. "You make them yourselves. You surround life with taboos, and then - you talk despairingly of the problems with which your own taboos alone have saddled you."

IX

At half-past nine one evening that week, Bertram was seated in his sitting-room at Miss Blake's lodgings, making entries, as usual, on the subject of taboo in his big black notebook. It was a large bare room, furnished with the customary round rosewood centre table, and decorated by a pair of green china vases, a set of wax flowers under a big glass shade, and a picture representing two mythical beings, with women's faces and birds' wings, hovering over the figure of a sleeping baby. Suddenly a hurried knock at the door attracted his attention. "Come in," he said softly, in that gentle and almost deferential voice which he used alike to his equals and to the lodging-house servant. The door opened at once, and Frida entered.

She was pale as a ghost, and she stepped light with a terrified tread. Bertram could see at a glance she was profoundly agitated. For a moment he could hardly imagine the reason why: then he remembered all at once the strict harem rules by which married women in England are hemmed in and circumvented. To visit an unmarried man alone by night is contrary to tribal usage. He rose, and advanced towards his visitor with outstretched arms. "Why, Frida," he cried, - "Mrs. Monteith - no, Frida - what's the matter? What has happened since I left? You look so pale and startled."

Frida closed the door cautiously, flung herself down into a chair in a despairing attitude, and buried her face in her hands for some moments in silence. "O Mr. Ingledew," she cried at last, looking up in an agony of shame and doubt: "Bertram - I KNOW it's wrong; I KNOW it's wicked; I ought never to have come. Robert would kill me if he found out. But it's my one last chance, and I couldn't BEAR not to say good-bye to you - just this once - for ever."

Bertram gazed at her in astonishment. Long and intimately as he had lived among the various devotees of divine taboos the whole world over, it was with difficulty still he could recall, each time, each particular restriction of the various systems. Then it came home to him with a rush. He removed the poor girl's hands gently from her face, which she had buried once more in them for pure shame, and held them in his own. "Dear Frida," he said tenderly, stroking them as he spoke, "why, what does all this mean? What's this sudden thunderbolt? You've come here to-night without your husband's leave, and you're afraid he'll discover you?"

Frida spoke under her breath, in a voice half-choked with frequent sobs. "Don't talk too loud," she whispered. "Miss Blake doesn't know I'm here. If she did, she'd tell on me. I slipped in quietly through the open back door. But I felt I MUST - I really, really MUST. I COULDN'T stop away; I COULDN'T help it."

Bertram gazed at her, distressed. Her tone was distressing. Horror and indignation for a moment overcame him. She had had to slip in there like a fugitive or a criminal. She had had to crawl away by stealth from that man, her keeper. She, a grown woman and a moral agent, with a will of her own and a heart and a conscience, was held so absolutely in serfdom as a particular man's thrall and chattel, that she could not even go out to visit a friend without these degrading subterfuges of creeping in unperceived by a back entrance, and talking low under her breath, lest a lodging-house crone should find out what she was doing. And all the world of England was so banded in league with the slave-driver against the soul he enslaved, that if Miss Blake had seen her she could hardly have come in: while, once in, she must tremble and whisper and steal about with muffled feet, for fear of discovery in this innocent adventure. He held his breath with stifled wrath. It was painful and degrading.

But he had no time just then to think much of all this, for there sat Frida, tremulous and shivering before his very eyes, trying hard to hide her beautiful white face in her quivering hands, and murmuring over and over again in a very low voice, like an agonised creature, "I couldn't BEAR not to be allowed to say good-bye to you for ever."

Bertram smoothed her cheek gently. She tried to prevent him, but he went on in spite of her, with a man's strong persistence. Notwithstanding his gentleness he was always virile. "Good-bye!" he cried. "Good-bye! why on earth good-bye, Frida? When I left you before dinner you never said one word of it to me."

"Oh, no," Frida cried, sobbing. "It's all Robert, Robert! As soon as ever you were gone, he called me into the library - which always means he's going to talk over some dreadful business with me - and he said to me,

'Frida, I've just heard from Phil that this man Ingledew, who's chosen to foist himself upon us, holds opinions and sentiments which entirely unfit him from being proper company for any lady. Now, he's been coming here a great deal too often of late. Next time he calls, I wish you to tell Martha you're not at home to him.'"

Bertram looked across at her with a melting look in his honest blue eyes. "And you came round to tell me of it, you dear thing!" he cried, seizing her hand and grasping it hard. "O Frida, how kind of you!"

Frida trembled from head to foot. The blood throbbed in her pulse. "Then you're not vexed with me," she sobbed out, all tremulous with gladness.

"Vexed with you! O Frida, how could I be vexed? You poor child! I'm so pleased, so glad, so grateful!"

Frida let her hand rest unresisting in his. "But, Bertram," she murmured, - "I MUST call you Bertram - I couldn't help it, you know. I like you so much, I couldn't let you go for ever without just saying good-bye to you."

"You DON'T like me; you LOVE me," Bertram answered with masculine confidence. "No, you needn't blush, Frida; you can't deceive me. . . . My darling, you love me, and you know I love you. Why should we two make any secret about our hearts any longer?" He laid his hand on her face again, making it tingle with joy. "Frida," he said solemnly, "you don't love that man you call your husband. . . . You haven't loved him for years. . . . You never really loved him."

There was something about the mere sound of

Bertram's calm voice that made Frida speak the truth more plainly and frankly than she could ever have spoken it to any ordinary Englishman. Yet she hung down her head, even so, and hesitated slightly. "Just at first," she murmured half-inaudibly, "I used to THINK I loved him. At any rate, I was pleased and flattered he should marry me."

"Pleased and flattered!" Bertram exclaimed, more to himself than to her; "great Heavens, how incredible! Pleased and flattered by that man! One can hardly conceive it! But you've never loved him since, Frida. You can't look me in the face and tell me you love him."

"No, not since the first few months," Frida answered, still hanging her head. "But, Bertram, he's my husband, and of course I must obey him."

"You must do nothing of the sort," Bertram cried authoritatively. "You don't love him at all, and you mustn't pretend to. It's wrong: it's wicked. Sooner or later - " He checked himself. "Frida," he went on, after a moment's pause, "I won't speak to you of what I was going to say just now. I'll wait a bit till you're stronger and better able to understand it. But there must be no more silly talk of farewells between us. I won't allow it. You're mine now - a thousand times more truly mine than ever you were Monteith's; and I can't do without you. You must go back to your husband for the present, I suppose, - the circumstances compel it, though I don't approve of it; but you must see me again . . . and soon . . . and often, just the same as usual. I won't go to your house, of course: the house is Monteith's; and everywhere among civilised and rational races the sanctity of the home is rightly respected. But YOU yourself he has no claim or right to taboo; and if *I* can help it, he shan't taboo you. You may go home now to-night, dear one; but you must meet me often. If you can't come round to my rooms - for fear of Miss Blake's fetich, the respectability of her house - we must meet elsewhere, till I can make fresh arrangements."

Frida gazed up at him in doubt. "But will it be RIGHT, Bertram?" she murmured.

The man looked down into her big eyes in dazed astonishment. "Why, Frida," he cried, half-pained at the question, "do you think if it were WRONG I'd advise you to do it? I'm here to help you, to guide you, to lead you on by degrees to higher and truer life. How can you imagine I'd ask you to do anything on earth unless I felt perfectly sure and convinced it was the very most right and proper conduct?"

His arm stole round her waist and drew her tenderly towards him. Frida allowed the caress passively. There was a robust frankness about his love-making that seemed to rob it of all taint or tinge of evil. Then he caught her bodily in his arms like a man who has never associated the purest and noblest of human passions with any lower thought, any baser personality. He had not taken his first lessons in the art of love from the wearied lips of joyless courtesans whom his own kind had debased and unsexed and degraded out of all semblance of womanhood. He bent over the woman of his choice and kissed her with chaste warmth. On the forehead first, then, after a short interval, twice on the lips. At each kiss, from which she somehow did not shrink, as if recognising its purity, Frida felt a strange thrill course through and through her. She quivered from head to foot. The scales fell from her eyes. The taboos of her race grew null and void within her. She looked up at him more boldly. "O Bertram," she whispered, nestling close to his side, and burying her blushing face in the man's curved bosom, "I don't know what you've done to me, but I feel quite different - as if I'd eaten the fruit of the tree of knowledge of good and evil."

"I hope you have," Bertram answered, in a very solemn voice; "for, Frida, you will need it." He pressed her close against his breast; and Frida Monteith, a free woman at last, clung there many minutes with no vile inherited sense of shame or wrongfulness. "I can't bear to go," she cried, still clinging to him and clutching him tight. "I'm so happy here, Bertram; oh, so happy, so happy!"

"Then why go away at all?" Bertram asked, quite simply.

Frida drew back in horror. "Oh, I must," she said, coming to herself: "I must, of course, because of Robert."

Bertram held her hand, smoothing it all the while with his own, as he mused and hesitated. "Well, it's clearly wrong to go back," he said, after a moment's pause. "You ought never, of course, to spend another night with that man you don't love and should never have lived with. But I suppose that's only a counsel of perfection: too hard a saying for you to understand or follow for the present. You'd better go back, just to-night: and, as time moves on, I can arrange something else for you. But when shall I see you again? - for now you belong to me. I sealed you with that kiss. When will you come and see me?"

"I can't come here, you know," Frida whispered, half-terrified; "for if I did, Miss Blake would see me."

Bertram smiled a bitter smile to himself. "So she would," he said, musing. "And though she's not the least interested in keeping up Robert Monteith's proprietary claim on your life and freedom, I'm beginning to understand now that it would be an offence against that mysterious and incomprehensible entity they call RESPECTABILITY if she were to allow me to receive you in her rooms. It's all very curious. But, of course, while I remain, I must be content to submit to it. By-and-by, perhaps, Frida, we two may manage to escape together from this iron generation. Meanwhile, I shall go up to London less often for the present, and you can come and meet me, dear, in the Middle Mill Fields at two o'clock on Monday."

She gazed up at him with perfect trust in those luminous dark eyes of hers. "I will, Bertram," she said firmly. She knew not herself what his kiss had done for her; but one thing she knew: from the moment their lips met, she had felt and understood in a flood of vision that perfect love which casteth out fear, and was no longer afraid of him.

"That's right, darling," the man answered, stooping down and laying his cheek against her own once more. "You are mine, and I am yours. You are not and never were Robert Monteith's, my Frida. So now, good-night, till Monday at two, beside the stile in Middle Mill Meadows!"

She clung to him for a moment in a passionate embrace. He let her stop there, while he smoothed her dark hair with one free hand. Then suddenly, with a burst, the older feelings of her race overcame her for a minute; she broke from his grasp and hid her head, all crimson, in a cushion on the sofa. One second later, again, she lifted her face unabashed. The new impulse stirred her. "I'm proud I love you, Bertram," she cried, with red lips and flashing eyes; "and I'm proud you love me!"

With that, she slipped quietly out, and walked, erect and graceful, no longer ashamed, down the lodging-house passage.

X

When she returned, Robert Monteith sat asleep over his paper in his easy-chair. It was his wont at night when he returned from business. Frida cast one contemptuous glance as she passed at his burly, unintelligent form, and went up to her bedroom.

But all that night long she never slept. Her head was too full of Bertram Ingledew.

Yet, strange to say, she felt not one qualm of conscience for their stolen meeting. No feminine terror, no fluttering fear, disturbed her equanimity. It almost seemed to her as if Bertram's kiss had released her by magic, at once and for ever, from the taboos of her nation. She had slipped out from home unperceived, that night, in fear and trembling, with many sinkings of heart and dire misgivings, while Robert and Phil were downstairs in the smoking-room; she had slunk round, crouching low, to Miss Blake's lodgings: and she had terrified her soul on the way with a good woman's doubts and a good woman's fears as to the wrongfulness of her attempt to say good-bye to the friend she might now no longer mix with. But from the moment her lips and Bertram's touched, all fear and doubt seemed utterly to have vanished; she lay there all night in a fierce ecstasy of love, hugging herself for strange delight, thinking only of Bertram, and wondering what manner of thing was this promised freedom whereof her lover had spoken to her so confidently. She trusted him now; she knew he would do right, and right alone: whatever he advised, she would be safe in following.

Next day, Robert went up to town to business as usual. He was immersed in palm-oil. By a quarter to two, Frida found herself in the fields. But, early as she went to fulfil her tryst, Bertram was there before her. He took her hand in his with a gentle pressure, and Frida felt a quick thrill she had never before experienced course suddenly through her. She looked around to right and left, to see if they were observed. Bertram noticed the instinctive movement. "My darling," he said in a low voice, "this is intolerable, unendurable. It's an insult not to be borne that you and I can't walk together in the fields of England without being subjected thus to such a many-headed espionage. I shall have to arrange something before long so as to see you at leisure. I can't be so bound by all the taboos of your country."

She looked up at him trustfully. "As you will, Bertram," she answered, without a moment's hesitation. "I know I'm yours now. Let it be what it may, I can do what you tell me."

He looked at her and smiled. He saw she was pure woman. He had met at last with a sister soul. There was a long, deep silence.

Frida was the first to break it with words. "Why do you always call them taboos, Bertram?" she asked at last, sighing.

"Why, Frida, don't you see?" he said, walking on through the deep grass. "Because they ARE taboos; that's the only reason. Why not give them their true name? We call them nothing else among my own people. All taboos are the same in origin and spirit, whether savage or civilised, eastern or western. You must see that now: for I know you are emancipated. They begin with belief in some fetich or bogey or other non-existent supernatural being; and they mostly go on to regard certain absolutely harmless - nay, sometimes even praiseworthy or morally obligatory - acts as proscribed by him and sure to be visited with his condign displeasure. So South Sea Islanders think, if they eat some particular luscious fruit tabooed for the chiefs, they'll be instantly struck dead by the mere power of the taboo in it; and English people think, if they go out in the country for a picnic on a tabooed day, or use certain harmless tabooed names and words, or inquire into the historical validity of certain incredible ancient documents, accounted sacred, or even dare to think certain things that no reasonable man can prevent himself from thinking, they'll be burned for ever in eternal fire for it. The common element is the dread of an unreal sanction. So in Japan and West Africa the people believe the whole existence of the world and the universe is bound up with the health of their own particular king or the safety of their own particular royal family; and therefore they won't allow their Mikado or their chief to go outside his palace, lest he should knock his royal foot against a stone, and so prevent the sun from shining and the rain from falling. In other places, it's a tree or a shrub with which the stability and persistence of the world is bound up; whenever that tree or shrub begins to droop or wither, the whole population rushes out in bodily fear and awe, bearing water to pour upon it, and crying aloud with wild cries as if their lives were in danger. If any man were to injure the tree, which of course is no more valuable than any other bush of its sort, they'd tear him to pieces on the spot, and kill or torture every member of his family. And so too, in England, most people believe, without a shadow of reason, that if men and women were allowed to manage their own personal relations, free from tribal interference, all life and order would go to rack and ruin; the world would become one vast, horrible orgy; and society would dissolve in some incredible fashion. To prevent this imaginary and impossible result, they insist upon regulating one another's lives from outside with the strictest taboos, like those which hem round the West African kings, and punish with cruel and relentless heartlessness every man, and still more every woman, who dares to transgress them."

"I think I see what you mean," Frida answered, blushing.

"And I mean it in the very simplest and most literal sense," Bertram went on quite seriously. "I'd been among you some time before it began to dawn on me that you English didn't regard your own taboos as essentially identical with other people's. To me, from the very first, they seemed absolutely the same as the similar taboos of Central Africans and South Sea Islanders. All of them spring alike from a common origin, the queer savage belief that various harmless or actually beneficial things may become at times in some mysterious way harmful and dangerous. The essence of them all lies in the erroneous idea that if certain contingencies occur, such as breaking an image or deserting a faith, some terrible evil will follow to one man or to the world, which evil, as a matter of fact, there's no reason at all to dread in any way. Sometimes, as in ancient Rome, Egypt, Central Africa, and England, the whole of life gets enveloped at last in a perfect mist and labyrinth of taboos, a cobweb of conventions. The Flamen Dialis at Rome, you know, mightn't ride or even touch a horse; he mightn't see an army under arms; nor wear a ring that wasn't broken; nor have a knot in any part of his clothing. He mightn't eat wheaten flour or leavened bread; he mightn't look at or even mention by name such unlucky things as a goat, a dog, raw meat, haricot beans, or common ivy. He mightn't walk under a vine; the feet of his bed had to be daubed with mud; his hair could only be cut by a free man, and with a bronze knife; he was encased and surrounded, as it were, by endless petty restrictions and regulations and taboos - just like those that now surround so many men, and especially so many young women, here in England."

"And you think they arise from the same causes?" Frida said, half-hesitating: for she hardly knew whether it was not wicked to say so.

"Why, of course they do," Bertram answered confidently. "That's not matter of opinion now; it's matter of demonstration. The worst of them all in their present complicated state are the ones that concern marriage and the other hideous sex-taboos. They seem to have been among the earliest human abuses; for marriage arises from the stone-age practice of felling a woman of another tribe with a blow of one's club, and dragging her off by the hair of her head to one's own cave as a slave and drudge; and they are still the most persistent and cruel of any - so much so, that your own people, as you know, taboo even the fair and free discussion of this the most important and serious question of life and morals. They make it, as we would say at home, a refuge for enforced ignorance. For it's well known that early tribes hold the most superstitious ideas about the relation of men to women, and dread the most ridiculous and impossible evils resulting from it; and these absurd terrors of theirs seem to have been handed on intact to civilised races, so that for fear of I know not what ridiculous bogey of their own imaginations, or dread of some unnatural restraining deity, men won't even discuss a matter of so much importance to them all, but, rather than let the taboo of silence be broken, will allow such horrible things to take place in their midst as I have seen with my eyes for these last six or seven weeks in your cities. O Frida, you can't imagine what things - for I know they hide them from you: cruelties of lust and neglect and shame such as you couldn't even dream of; women dying of foul disease, in want and dirt deliberately forced upon them by the will of your society; destined beforehand for death, a hateful lingering death - a death more disgusting than aught you can conceive - in order that the rest of you may be safely tabooed, each a maid intact, for the man who weds her. It's the hatefullest taboo of all the hateful taboos I've ever seen on my wanderings, the unworthiest of a pure or moral community."

He shut his eyes as if to forget the horrors of which he spoke. They were fresh and real to him. Frida did not like to question him further. She knew to what he referred, and in a dim, vague way (for she was less wise than he, she knew) she thought she could imagine why he found it all so terrible.

They walked on in silence a while through the deep, lush grass of the July meadow. At last Bertram spoke again: "Frida," he said, with a trembling quiver, "I didn't sleep last night. I was thinking this thing over - this question of our relations."

"Nor did I," Frida answered, thrilling through, responsive. "I was thinking the same thing. . . . And, Bertram, 'twas the happiest night I ever remember."

Bertram's face flushed rosy red, that native colour of triumphant love; but he answered nothing. He only looked at her with a look more eloquent by far than a thousand speeches.

"Frida," he went on at last, "I've been thinking it all over; and I feel, if only you can come away with me for just seven days, I could arrange at the end of that time - to take you home with me."

Frida's face in turn waxed rosy red; but she answered only in a very low voice: "Thank you, Bertram."

"Would you go with me?" Bertram cried, his face aglow with pleasure. "You know, it's a very, very long way off; and I can't even tell you where it is or how you get there. But can you trust me enough to try? Are you not afraid to come with me?"

Frida's voice trembled slightly.

"I'm not afraid, if that's all," she answered in a very firm tone. "I love you, and I trust you, and I could follow you to the world's end - or, if needful, out of it. But there's one other question. Bertram, ought I to?"

She asked it, more to see what answer Bertram would make to her than from any real doubt; for ever since that kiss last night, she felt sure in her own mind with a woman's certainty whatever Bertram told her was the thing she ought to do; but she wanted to know in what light he regarded it.

Bertram gazed at her hard.

"Why, Frida," he said, "it's right, of course, to go. The thing that's WRONG is to stop with that man one minute longer than's absolutely necessary. You don't love him - you never loved him; or, if you ever did, you've long since ceased to do so. Well, then, it's a dishonour to yourself to spend one more day with him. How can you submit to the hateful endearments of a man you don't love or care for? How wrong to yourself, how infinitely more wrong to your still unborn and unbegotten children! Would you consent to become the mother of sons and daughters by a man whose whole character is utterly repugnant to you? Nature has given us this divine instinct of love within, to tell us with what persons we should spontaneously unite: will you fly in her face and unite with a man whom you feel and know to be wholly unworthy of you? With us, such conduct would be considered disgraceful. We think every man and woman should be free to do as they will with their own persons; for that is the very basis and foundation of personal liberty. But if any man or woman were openly to confess they yielded their persons to another for any other reason than because the strongest sympathy and love compelled them, we should silently despise them. If you don't love Monteith, it's your duty to him, and still more your duty to yourself and your unborn children, at once to leave him; if you DO love me, it's your duty to me, and still more your duty to yourself and our unborn children, at once to cleave to me. Don't let any sophisms of taboo-mongers come in to obscure that plain natural duty. Do right first; let all else go. For one of yourselves, a poet of your own, has said truly:

'Because right is right, to follow right
Were wisdom in the scorn of consequence.'"

Frida looked up at him with admiration in her big black eyes. She had found the truth, and the truth had made her free.

"O Bertram," she cried with a tremor, "it's good to be like you. I felt from the very first how infinitely you differed from the men about me. You seemed so much greater and higher and nobler. How grateful I ought to be to Robert Monteith for having spoken to me yesterday and forbidden me to see you! for if he hadn't, you might never have kissed me last night, and then I might never have seen things as I see them at present."

There was another long pause; for the best things we each say to the other are said in the pauses. Then Frida relapsed once more into speech: "But what about the children?" she asked rather timidly.

Bertram looked puzzled. "Why, what about the children?" he repeated in a curious way. "What difference on earth could that make to the children?"

"Can I bring them with me, I mean?" Frida asked, a little tremulous for the reply. "I couldn't bear to leave them. Even for you, dear Bertram, I could never desert them."

Bertram gazed at her dismayed. "Leave them!" he cried. "Why, Frida, of course you could never leave them. Do you mean to say anybody would be so utterly unnatural, even in England, as to separate a mother from her own children?"

"I don't think Robert would let me keep them," Frida faltered, with tears in her eyes; "and if he didn't, the law, of course, would take his side against me."

"Of course!" Bertram answered, with grim sarcasm in his face, "of course! I might have guessed it. If there IS an injustice or a barbarity possible, I might have been sure the law of England would make haste to perpetrate it. But you needn't fear, Frida. Long before the law of England could be put in motion, I'll have completed my arrangements for taking you - and them too - with me. There are advantages sometimes even in the barbaric delay of what your lawyers are facetiously pleased to call justice."

"Then I may bring them with me?" Frida cried, flushing red.

Bertram nodded assent. "Yes," he said, with grave gentleness. "You may bring them with you. And as soon as you like, too. Remember, dearest, every night you pass under that creature's roof, you commit the vilest crime a woman can commit against her own purity."

XI

Never in her life had Frida enjoyed anything so much as those first four happy days at Heymoor. She had come away with Bertram exactly as Bertram himself desired her to do, without one thought of anything on earth except to fulfil the higher law of her own nature; and she was happy in her intercourse with the one man who could understand it, the one man who had waked it to its fullest pitch, and could make it resound sympathetically to his touch in every chord and every fibre. They had chosen a lovely spot on a heather-clad moorland, where she could stroll alone with Bertram among the gorse and ling, utterly oblivious of Robert Monteith and the unnatural world she had left for ever behind her. Her soul drank in deep draughts of the knowledge of good and evil from Bertram's lips; she felt it was indeed a privilege to be with him and listen to him; she wondered how she could ever have endured that old bad life with the lower man who was never her equal, now she had once tasted and known what life can be when two well-matched souls walk it together, abreast, in holy fellowship.

The children, too, were as happy as the day was long. The heath was heaven to them. They loved Bertram well, and were too young to be aware of anything unusual in the fact of his accompanying them. At the little inn on the hill-top where they stopped to lodge, nobody asked any compromising questions: and Bertram felt so sure he could soon complete his arrangements for taking Frida and the children "home," as he still always phrased it, that Frida had no doubts for their future happiness. As for Robert Monteith, that bleak, cold man, she hardly even remembered him: Bertram's first kiss seemed almost to have driven the very memory of her husband clean out of her consciousness. She only regretted, now she had left him, the false and mistaken sense of duty which had kept her so long tied to an inferior soul she could never love, and did wrong to marry.

And all the time, what strange new lessons, what beautiful truths, she learned from Bertram! As they strolled together, those sweet August mornings, hand locked in hand, over the breezy upland, what new insight he gave her into men and things! what fresh impulse he supplied to her keen moral nature! The misery and wrong of the world she lived in came home to her now in deeper and blacker hues than ever she had conceived it in: and with that consciousness came also the burning desire of every wakened soul to right and redress it. With Bertram by her side, she felt she could not even harbour an unholy wish or admit a wrong feeling; that vague sense of his superiority, as of a higher being, which she had felt from the very first moment she met him at Brackenhurst, had deepened and grown more definite now by closer intercourse; and she recognised that what she had fallen in love with from the earliest beginning was the beauty of holiness shining clear in his countenance. She had chosen at last the better part, and she felt in her soul that, come what might, it could not be taken away from her.

In this earthly paradise of pure love, undefiled, she spent three full days and part of another. On the morning of the fourth, she sent the country girl they had engaged to take care of the children, out on the moor with the little ones, while she herself and Bertram went off alone, past the barrow that overlooks the Devil's Saucepan, and out on the open ridge that stretches with dark growth of heath and bracken far away into the misty blue distance of Hampshire. Bertram had just been speaking to her, as they sat on the dry sand, of the buried chieftain whose bones still lay hid under that grass-grown barrow, and of the slaughtered wives whose bodies slept beside him, massacred in cold blood to accompany their dead lord to the world of shadows. He had been contrasting these hideous slaveries of taboo-ridden England, past or present, with the rational freedom of his own dear country, whither he hoped so soon with good luck to take her, when suddenly Frida raised her eager eyes from the ground, and saw somebody or something coming across the moor from eastward in their direction.

All at once, a vague foreboding of evil possessed her. Hardly quite knowing why, she felt this approaching object augured no good to their happiness. "Look, Bertram," she cried, seizing his arm in her fright, "there's somebody coming."

Bertram raised his eyes and looked. Then he shaded them with his hands. "How strange!" he said simply, in his candid way: "it looks for all the world just like the man who was once your husband!"

Frida rose in alarm. "Oh, what can we do?" she cried, wringing her hands. "What ever can we do? It's he!

It's Robert!"

"Surely he can't have come on purpose!" Bertram exclaimed, taken aback. "When he sees us, he'll turn aside. He must know of all people on earth he's the one least likely at such a time to be welcome. He can't want to disturb the peace of another man's honeymoon!"

But Frida, better used to the savage ways of the world she had always lived in, made answer, shrinking and crouching, "He's hunted us down, and he's come to fight you."

"To fight me!" Bertram exclaimed. "Oh, surely not that! I was told by those who ought best to know, you English had got far beyond the stage of private war and murderous vendetta."

"For everything else," Frida answered, cowering down in her terror of her husband's vengeance, not for herself indeed so much as for Bertram. "For everything else, we have; but NOT for a woman."

There was no time just then, however, for further explanation of this strange anomaly. Monteith had singled them out from a great distance with his keen, clear sight, inherited from generations of Highland ancestors, and now strode angrily across the moor, with great wrathful steps, in his rival's direction. Frida nestled close to Bertram, to protect her from the man to whom her country's laws and the customs of her tribe would have handed her over blindfold. Bertram soothed her with his hand, and awaited in silence, with some dim sense of awe, the angry barbarian's arrival.

He came up very quickly, and stood full in front of

them, glaring with fierce eyes at the discovered lovers. For a minute or two his rage would not allow him to speak, nor even to act; he could but stand and scowl from under his brows at Bertram. But after a long pause his wrath found words. "You infernal scoundrel!" he burst forth, "so at last I've caught you! How dare you sit there and look me straight in the face? You infernal thief, how dare you? how dare you?"

Bertram rose and confronted him. His own face, too, flushed slightly with righteous indignation; but he answered for all that in the same calm and measured tones as ever: "I am NOT a scoundrel, and I will not submit to be called so even by an angry savage. I ask you in return, how dare you follow us? You must have known your presence would be very unwelcome. I should have thought this was just the one moment in your life and the one place on earth where even YOU would have seen that to stop away was your imperative duty. Mere self-respect would dictate such conduct. This lady has given you clear proof indeed that your society and converse are highly distasteful to her."

Robert Monteith glared across at him with the face of a tiger. "You infamous creature," he cried, almost speechless with rage, "do you dare to defend my wife's adultery?"

Bertram gazed at him with a strange look of mingled horror and astonishment. "You poor wretch!" he answered, as calmly as before, but with evident contempt; "how can you dare, such a thing as you, to apply these vile words to your moral superiors? Adultery it was indeed, and untruth to her own higher and purer nature, for this lady to spend one night of her life under your roof with you; what she has taken now in exchange is holy marriage, the only real and sacred marriage, the marriage of true souls, to which even the wiser of yourselves, the poets of your nation, would not admit impediment. If you dare to apply such base language as this to my lady's actions, you must answer for it to me, her natural protector, for I will not permit it."

At the words, quick as lightning, Monteith pulled from his pocket a loaded revolver and pointed it full at his rival. With a cry of terror, Frida flung herself between them, and tried to protect her lover with the shield of her own body. But Bertram gently unwound her arms and held her off from him tenderly. "No, no, darling," he said slowly, sitting down with wonderful calm upon a big grey sarsen-stone that abutted upon the pathway; "I had forgotten again; I keep always forgetting what kind of savages I have to deal with. If I chose, I could snatch that murderous weapon from his hand, and shoot him dead with it in self-defence - for I'm stronger than he is. But if I did, what use? I could never take you home with me. And after all, what could we either of us do in the end in this bad, wild world of your fellow-countrymen? They would take me and hang me; and all would be up with you. For your sake, Frida, to shield you from the effects of their cruel taboos, there's but one course open: I must submit to this madman. He may shoot me if he will. . . . Stand free, and let him!"

But with a passionate oath, Robert Monteith seized her arm and flung her madly from him. She fell, reeling, on one side. His eyes were bloodshot with the savage thirst for vengeance. He raised the deadly weapon. Bertram Ingledew, still seated on the big round boulder, opened his breast in silence to receive the bullet. There was a moment's pause. For that moment, even Monteith himself, in his maniac mood, felt dimly aware of that mysterious restraining power all the rest who knew him had so often felt in their dealings with the Alien. But it was only for a moment. His coarser nature was ill adapted to recognise that ineffable air as of a superior being that others observed in him. He pulled the trigger and fired. Frida gave one loud shriek of despairing horror. Bertram's body fell back on the bare heath behind it.

XII

Mad as he was with jealousy, that lowest and most bestial of all the vile passions man still inherits from the ape and tiger, Robert Monteith was yet quite sane enough to know in his own soul what deed he had wrought, and in what light even his country's barbaric laws would regard his action. So the moment he had wreaked to the full his fiery vengeance on the man who had never wronged him, he bent over the body with strangely eager eyes, expecting to see upon it some evidence of his guilt, some bloody mark of the hateful crime his own hand had committed. At the same instant, Frida, recovering from his blow that had sent her reeling, rushed frantically forward, flung herself with wild passion on her lover's corpse, and covered the warm lips with hot, despairing kisses.

One marvellous fact, however, impressed them both with a vague sense of the unknown and the mysterious from the very first second. No spot nor trace of blood marred the body anywhere. And, even as they looked, a strange perfume, as of violets or of burning incense, began by degrees to flood the moor around them. Then slowly, while they watched, a faint blue flame seemed to issue from the wound in Bertram's right side and rise lambent into the air above the murdered body. Frida drew back and gazed at it, a weird thrill of mystery and unconscious hope beguiling for one moment her profound pang of bereavement. Monteith, too, stood away a pace or two, in doubt and surprise, the deep consciousness of some strange and unearthly power overawing for a while even his vulgar and commonplace Scotch bourgeois nature. Gradually, as they gazed, the pale blue flame, rising higher and higher, gathered force and volume, and the perfume as of violets became distinct on the air, like the savour of a purer life than this century wots of. Bit by bit, the wan blue light, flickering thicker and thicker, shaped itself into the form and features of a man, even the outward semblance of Bertram Ingledew. Shadowy, but transfigured with an ineffable glory, it hovered for a minute or two above the spot on the moor where the corpse had lain; for now they were aware that as the flame-shape formed, the body that lay dead upon the ground beneath dissolved by degrees and melted into it. Not a trace was left on the heath of Robert Monteith's crime: not a dapple of blood, not a clot of gore: only a pale blue flame and a persistent image represented the body that was once Bertram Ingledew's.

Again, even as they looked, a still weirder feeling began to creep over them. The figure, growing fainter, seemed to fade away piecemeal in the remote distance. But it was not in space that it faded; it appeared rather to become dim in some vaguer and far more mysterious fashion, like the memories of childhood or the aching abysses of astronomical calculation. As it slowly dissolved, Frida stretched out her hands to it with a wild cry, like the cry of a mother for her first-born. "O Bertram," she moaned, "where are you going? Do you mean to leave me? Won't you save me from this man? Won't you take me home with you?"

Dim and hollow, as from the womb of time unborn, a

calm voice came back to her across the gulf of ages: "Your husband willed it, Frida, and the customs of your nation. You can come to me, but I can never return to you. In three days longer your probation would have been finished. But I forgot with what manner of savage I had still to deal. And now I must go back once more to the place whence I came - to THE TWENTY-FIFTH CENTURY."

The voice died away in the dim recesses of the future. The pale blue flame flickered forward and vanished. The shadowy shape melted through an endless vista of to-morrows. Only the perfume as of violets or of a higher life still hung heavy upon the air, and a patch of daintier purple burned bright on the moor, like a pool of crimson blood, where the body had fallen. Only that, and a fierce ache in Frida's tortured heart; only that, and a halo of invisible glory round the rich red lips, where his lips had touched them.

XIII

Frida seated herself in her misery on the ice-worn boulder where three minutes earlier Bertram had been sitting. Her face was buried in her bloodless hands. All the world grew blank to her.

Monteith, for his part, sat down a little way off with folded arms on another sarsen-stone, fronting her. The strange and unearthly scene they had just passed through impressed him profoundly. For the first few minutes a great horror held him. But his dogged Scottish nature still brooded over his wrongs, in spite of the terrible sight he had so unexpectedly evoked. In a way, he felt he had had his revenge; for had he not drawn upon his man, and fired at him and killed him? Still, after the fever and torment of the last few days, it was a relief to find, after all, he was not, as this world would judge, a murderer. Man and crime were alike mere airy phantoms. He could go back now to the inn and explain with a glib tongue how Mr. Ingledew had been hurriedly called away to town on important business. There was no corpse on the moor, no blabbing blood to tell the story of his attempted murder: nobody anywhere, he felt certain in his own stolid soul, would miss the mysterious Alien who came to them from beyond the distant abyss of centuries. With true Scotch caution, indeed, even in the midst of his wrath, Robert Monteith had never said a word to any one at Brackenhurst of how his wife had left him. He was too proud a man, if it came to that, to acknowledge what seemed to him a personal disgrace, till circumstances should absolutely force such acknowledgment upon him. He had glossed it over meanwhile with the servants and neighbours by saying that Mrs. Monteith had gone away with the children for their accustomed holiday as always in August. Frida had actually chosen the day appointed for their seaside journey as the fittest moment for her departure with Bertram, so his story was received without doubt or inquiry. He had bottled up his wrath in his own silent soul. There was still room, therefore, to make all right again at home in the eyes of the world - if but Frida was willing. So he sat there long, staring hard at his wife in speechless debate, and discussing with himself whether or not to make temporary overtures of peace to her.

In this matter, his pride itself fought hard with his pride. That is the wont of savages. Would it not be better, now Bertram Ingledew had fairly disappeared for ever from their sphere, to patch up a hollow truce for a time at least with Frida, and let all things be to the outer eye exactly as they had always been? The bewildering and brain-staggering occurrences of the last half-hour, indeed, had struck deep and far into his hard Scotch nature. The knowledge that the man who had stolen his wife from him (as he phrased it to himself in his curious belated mediaeval phraseology) was not a real live man of flesh and blood at all, but an evanescent phantom of the twenty-fifth century, made him all the more ready to patch up for the time-being a nominal reconciliation. His nerves - for even HE had nerves - were still trembling to the core with the mystic events of that wizard morning; but clearer and clearer still it dawned upon him each moment that if things were ever to be set right at all they must be set right then and there, before he returned to the inn, and before Frida once more went back to their children. To be sure, it was Frida's place to ask forgiveness first, and make the first advances. But Frida made no move. So after sitting there long, salving his masculine vanity with the flattering thought that after all his rival was no mere man at all, but a spirit, an avatar, a thing of pure imagination, he raised his head at last and looked inquiringly towards Frida.

"Well?" he said slowly.

Frida raised her head from her hands and gazed across at him scornfully.

"I was thinking," Monteith began, feeling his way with caution, but with a magnanimous air, "that perhaps - after all - for the children's sake, Frida -"

With a terrible look, his wife rose up and fronted him. Her face was red as fire; her heart was burning. She spoke with fierce energy. "Robert Monteith," she said firmly, not even deigning to treat him as one who had once been her husband, "for the children's sake, or for my own sake, or for any power on earth, do you think, poor empty soul, after I've spent three days of my life with HIM, I'd ever spend three hours again with YOU? If you do, then this is all: murderer that you are, you mistake my nature."

And turning on her heel, she moved slowly away towards the far edge of the moor with a queenly gesture.

Monteith followed her up a step or two. She turned and waved him back. He stood glued to the ground, that weird sense of the supernatural once more overcoming him. For some seconds he watched her without speaking a word. Then at last he broke out. "What are you going to do, Frida?" he asked, almost anxiously.

Frida turned and glanced back at him with scornful eyes. Her mien was resolute. The revolver with which he had shot Bertram Ingledew lay close by her feet, among the bracken on the heath, where Monteith had flung it. She picked it up with one hand, and once more waved him backward.

"I'm going to follow him," she answered solemnly, in a very cold voice, "where YOU have sent him. But alone by myself: not here, before you." And she brushed him away, as he tried to seize it, with regal dignity.

Monteith, abashed, turned back without one word, and made his way to the inn in the little village. But Frida walked on by herself, in the opposite direction, across the open moor and through the purple heath, towards black despair and the trout-ponds at Broughton.

www.ingramcontent.com/pod-product-compliance
Lightning Source LLC
LaVergne TN
LVHW091248110826
845146LV00001BA/365

* 9 7 8 1 4 2 1 8 0 1 3 6 0 *